Echoes of Atlantis

Zephyr Wrenwood

Published by Solstice Skylancer, 2023.

ECHOES OF ATLANTIS

First edition. September 30, 2023.

Copyright © 2023 Zephyr Wrenwood.

ISBN: 979-8223606826

Written by Zephyr Wrenwood.

Table of Contents

Chapter One: The Clock's Secret

Lia's fingers brushed over the delicate parchment, her hazel eyes narrowing at the peculiar symbols etched onto its surface. The attic was filled with forgotten relics, but this old map, yellowed by age and concealed beneath dusty books and broken toys, had caught her attention. The map was a puzzle waiting to be solved, with cryptic annotations and intricate details that hinted at a hidden world.

Outside her window, the Oregon rain tapped gently against the glass, filling the attic with its rhythmic melody. But the stormy weather didn't deter her focus; she was engrossed, tracing the lines leading to a mysterious coastal town—Synchronos.

"Honey, are you still in the attic?" called out her mother from the floor below. "Dinner's ready!"

Lia hesitated. The familiar aroma of her mother's lasagna wafted up, tempting her. But the map—it was like nothing she'd ever seen before. However, the growling of her stomach reminded her that mysteries could wait; for now, dinner couldn't.

Tucking the map under her arm, she carefully descended the narrow staircase, the old wood creaking under her weight.

As she stepped into the dining room, her younger brother, Jamie, glanced up from his plate, his face smeared with tomato sauce. "What took you so long? I got the bigger slice because you weren't here."

Lia smirked. "You always find a way, don't you?"

Their father chuckled. "He gets that from me." He winked at Jamie, who beamed with pride.

Dinner progressed with the usual chatter. Jamie regaled the family with tales of his adventures in the neighborhood—most of which involved his best friend, Rufus, and their mischievous plans gone awry. Their parents laughed and exchanged amused glances, savoring these fleeting moments of childhood innocence.

Yet, throughout dinner, Lia's mind kept drifting back to the map and its secrets.

After dessert, with the remnants of chocolate cake still clinging to their plates, Lia cleared her throat. "I found something interesting in the attic today."

She carefully unfolded the map, laying it out on the table. The intricate design and cryptic symbols drew her family's eyes instantly.

"What is it?" Jamie asked, his voice filled with curiosity.

"It looks like a map," her mother mused. "But of where?"

Lia pointed to the annotations. "It leads to a place called Synchronos, but I've never heard of it."

Her father leaned in, adjusting his glasses. "It looks old, perhaps centuries. This might be a historical map, Lia."

"But why was it hidden in our attic?" Lia asked.

Her mother shrugged. "Maybe it belonged to your great-grandfather. He was quite the explorer in his days."

Jamie's eyes sparkled with mischief. "What if it leads to buried treasure? Like in the movies!"

While the family entertained the idea, laughing and imagining what they'd do with a newfound fortune, Lia wasn't so sure. The map felt different—more profound. It was as if it was calling out to her, urging her to uncover its secrets.

Later that night, as the house settled into its nightly routine, the soft glow from Lia's desk lamp bathed her room in a warm light. She had a notebook spread open, jotting down notes and observations about the map.

The details on it were intricate. Some symbols resembled those she had come across in her history class, but others were entirely foreign. As she examined it closely, a pattern began to emerge—a series of numbers.

"It looks like... coordinates," she whispered to herself.

Grabbing her laptop, Lia began to search. The internet, with its vast expanse of knowledge, could surely offer some clue.

Hours slipped away as she delved into forums, read old manuscripts, and pieced together the fragments of information she could find. As dawn's first light began to filter through her curtains, Lia stumbled upon an old legend.

Synchronos, according to folklore, was a hidden coastal town. But it wasn't just any town—it was believed to be a place where time, tide, and truth intertwined. A place of magic and mysteries.

Eyes heavy with sleep but mind racing with excitement, Lia knew one thing for sure—this summer, she was going on an adventure to uncover the secrets of Synchronos.

And as she finally surrendered to sleep, dreams filled with ancient symbols, hidden towns, and the promise of adventure danced in her mind.

Lia awoke to the sound of Jamie's shouts from downstairs. She groggily checked her alarm clock and was surprised to find that it was already past 10 AM. The evening's research had taken its toll, but the mysteries of the map had proven too alluring to resist.

"Morning, sleepyhead," Jamie teased as she trudged downstairs. "Dream of treasures and mysterious towns?"

Lia playfully ruffled his hair. "If only you knew."

Their mother set a plate of pancakes in front of her. "You were up late," she noted with a raised eyebrow. "Found anything interesting about that map?"

Lia took a deep breath. "According to some old legends, Synchronos is more than just a town. It's a place where mysteries of time itself might be hidden."

Her father, engrossed in his morning paper, looked up with a smirk. "Sounds like something out of a movie, doesn't it?"

Jamie's eyes were wide. "You're not thinking of going there, are you?"

Before Lia could respond, their mother chimed in. "It's summer break, and if Lia wants an adventure, why not? As long as you're careful and keep us informed."

Lia beamed. "Thanks, Mom!"

Over the next few days, she began her preparations. Armed with the map, a notebook filled with her research, and a backpack of essentials, Lia was ready to embark on her journey. Jamie, filled with a mix of envy and concern, gifted her a small compass. "For direction," he had said with a shy smile.

The train ride to the nearest station to Synchronos was a long one. The rhythmic chug of the wheels and the blur of the passing landscape gave Lia plenty of time to think. The closer she got to her destination, the more she felt a strange pull, a sense of destiny.

Once she reached the station, she was hit by the salty tang of the sea. Synchronos was still a day's hike away, through winding coastal trails and dense forests. Lia relished the challenge, her boots kicking up the soft earth as she made her way through the woods.

As evening approached, she found herself on a hill overlooking the elusive town of Synchronos. The setting sun cast a golden hue over the buildings, and the town seemed to shimmer, as if it was slightly out of sync with the rest of the world.

She descended the hill and was soon walking on cobblestone streets. The town, though small, was bustling with activity. Children ran around playing, market vendors hawked their wares, and the air was filled with laughter and chatter. Yet, there was an undercurrent of something more, a palpable sense of history and mystery.

Intrigued by a sign that read "Inn of Times," Lia decided to check in for the night. The innkeeper, a middle-aged woman with streaks of silver in her hair, greeted her warmly. "We don't get many outsiders here," she said with a smile. "What brings you to Synchronos?"

Lia hesitated for a moment but then decided to share. "I found a map. An old one. It pointed me here."

The innkeeper's eyes widened slightly. "Ah, so you're seeking the truths of time," she murmured. "Well, you've come to the right place. But be wary, young traveler. Not all mysteries are meant to be unraveled."

With a key to her room and a heart full of curiosity, Lia settled in. The room was cozy, with walls lined with old books and paintings of the sea. One particular painting caught her eye. It depicted a boy, around her age, standing on a beach with a peculiar pendant around his neck. The pendant, shaped like an hourglass, seemed eerily familiar.

Unable to shake off the feeling, Lia decided to head to the town's library. The place was a treasure trove of information. Dusty tomes, ancient manuscripts, and stacks of parchment filled the room. An elderly librarian, Mr. Elmsworth, offered to help.

"I'm looking for any information on this," Lia said, showing him the map.

Mr. Elmsworth adjusted his spectacles, taking a closer look. "Ah, you've stumbled upon something rare, young lady. This map is said to have been crafted by the founders of Synchronos. It's believed that they had the power to manipulate time."

Lia's heart raced. "Is it true? Can time really be manipulated here?"

Mr. Elmsworth leaned in, lowering his voice. "There are places in Synchronos where time stands still, where minutes can stretch into hours and days can feel like moments. But," he added with a sigh, "such knowledge comes at a price."

Lia spent hours at the library, pouring over books and legends. She learned about the founders, a group of time-travelers, and their quest to create a safe haven from the ravages of time. She also came across mentions of a pendant, much like the one in the painting in her room, which was said to hold the key to Synchronos' secrets.

Exhausted but exhilarated, Lia returned to the inn. As she climbed into bed, her thoughts were a whirlwind of legends, time-travel, and the mysteries that lay ahead.

Outside her window, the town of Synchronos lay bathed in moonlight, its secrets waiting to be discovered. And Lia knew that her adventure was only just beginning.

Morning light seeped through the gossamer curtains of the Inn of Times, casting a soft, radiant glow on the wooden floors. The room was steeped in silence, save for the distant sound of gulls from the harbor. Lia, wrapped in the comfort of the blanket, stirred to consciousness.

The events of the previous evening felt like a dream—a dizzying array of stories and myths, whispers of time manipulation, and the enigmatic pendant in the portrait. She groggily sat up, her mind replaying the librarian's words. With renewed determination, Lia decided her first mission in Synchronos would be to find that pendant.

Her journey began at the heart of the town—a quaint square, bustling with activity. Children were playing hopscotch on the cobblestone, stalls overflowed with colorful fruits and trinkets, and the aroma of freshly baked bread permeated the air.

Lia approached a nearby stall, captivated by a collection of intricate, handmade necklaces. She wondered if she might find a replica or even the original pendant among these treasures.

An elderly lady, her skin sun-kissed and wrinkled, smiled warmly. "Looking for something special, dear?"

Hesitating briefly, Lia showed her the sketched image of the pendant she'd drawn from memory. "Have you seen something like this?"

The woman's eyes widened in recognition. "The Timekeeper's Amulet," she whispered, leaning closer. "It's been years since I've seen one. They say it has the power to harness the enigmatic energies of Synchronos."

Lia's heart skipped a beat. "Do you know where I can find it?"

The vendor sighed, her gaze distant. "The last known keeper of the amulet was a young lad named Kael. But that was decades ago, and no one has seen him in years. Some say he's still around, trapped in a time loop. Others believe he left Synchronos for good."

As Lia pondered this, a hand tugged at her sleeve. It was a boy, no older than Jamie. "If you're seeking Kael, the cliffs might have your answers."

"Cliffs?" Lia repeated, intrigued.

He nodded. "Every evening, just as the sun sets, a silhouette stands there, staring at the horizon. Some of us kids tried talking to him, but he seems lost in time."

Thanking the boy and the vendor, Lia made her way to the cliffs, the anticipation bubbling within her.

The cliffs of Synchronos provided a panoramic view of the vast, azure expanse of the sea. The rhythmic crash of waves against rocks played a mesmerizing tune, and the breeze carried whispers of age-old secrets.

As the sun began its descent, painting the sky in hues of gold and crimson, a silhouette emerged. The figure stood with an air of melancholic grace, his gaze fixed on the horizon. Lia's heart raced as she approached him.

"Kael?" she ventured.

The young man turned, surprise evident in his eyes. "Who are you?"

"I'm Lia. I came here in search of answers." She showed him the sketch of the pendant. "I believe you might have them."

Kael's expression shifted from surprise to understanding. He slowly revealed the amulet from beneath his shirt—a perfect match to Lia's sketch.

"This amulet," he began, his voice tinged with nostalgia, "was passed down through my family. It's believed to be tied to the very foundations of Synchronos."

Lia listened, rapt, as Kael spoke of his ancestors—the founders of Synchronos, their mastery over time, and the creation of the amulet as a safeguard.

"Over the years, many have sought its power," he continued, "But its true purpose remains a mystery. Even to me."

As the final rays of the sun vanished, plunging the horizon into twilight, Kael extended an invitation to Lia. "Tomorrow, there's a gathering at the town hall. Elders and Keepers of Synchronos' lore come together to discuss the town's mysteries. You should come."

Grateful, Lia nodded. "I'll be there."

That night, dreams of time loops, shimmering amulets, and shadowy figures filled her sleep. But intertwined with the enigma was a sense of purpose and destiny.

The next morning, the town hall—a grand building with tall spires and stained glass windows—was abuzz. Locals and a few outsiders, all drawn to Synchronos by tales of its enigma, filled the room.

Kael, standing at the podium, began the discussion. Stories were shared, theories debated, and ancient texts deciphered. Hours felt like minutes as the mysteries of Synchronos unfurled.

At the gathering's conclusion, an elder approached Lia. "You have the spirit of a seeker," he remarked, handing her a scroll. "This might guide you further."

The scroll contained an intricate puzzle—a series of clues and riddles pointing to various landmarks around Synchronos. The final piece, it hinted, would unveil the amulet's true purpose.

With Kael by her side, Lia embarked on this new quest. From deciphering symbols in the town's fountain to unearthing buried tokens at the old lighthouse, their journey was fraught with challenges. But each step brought them closer to the truth.

As days turned into weeks, Lia and Kael grew close, their bond forged in the fires of adventure and discovery. The town of Synchronos, with its quirks and mysteries, became a backdrop to their blossoming friendship.

Finally, at the culmination of their quest, they stood at the Heart of Synchronos—a hidden chamber deep beneath the town. Here, the energies of time converged. With the amulet in hand and the puzzle solved, they unlocked its secret.

The chamber illuminated, revealing a grand tapestry of time—a visualization of past, present, and potential futures. The amulet, they realized, was not just a tool but a bridge, connecting the bearer to the infinite possibilities of time.

As Lia and Kael emerged from the chamber, the town of Synchronos celebrated their discovery. The once-lost lore was now restored, and the Heart of Synchronos beat once more with vibrant energy.

Amidst the festivities, Lia and Kael shared a quiet moment, looking out at the sea. Their journey had not only unraveled the mysteries of Synchronos but had also forged a bond that transcended time.

"I'm glad our paths crossed, Lia," Kael murmured.

Lia smiled, holding up the amulet that had started it all. "Me too. It's funny how time works, isn't it?"

In the town of Synchronos, where time danced to its tune and mysteries lurked in every corner, two souls had found their destiny. And as the waves crashed against the cliffs, the stories of the past merged with hopes for the future, crafting tales for generations to come.

Chapter Two: Secrets of the Sea

Morning in Synchronos was always a unique experience. The town seemed to wake up in layers, the early risers mingling with those who appeared to be from another time altogether. It was as if the entire town was caught in a gentle ebb and flow of time, reminiscent of the tide.

Lia found herself at the docks, mesmerized by the boats swaying in harmony with the waves. The fishermen, with their rugged faces and tales of the sea, were preparing for their day. Seagulls cawed overhead, soaring with an elegance that seemed almost choreographed.

"Lia!" called a familiar voice. Turning around, she saw Jamie, out of breath and looking completely out of place amidst the seasoned sailors. His eyes, wide with a mix of excitement and anxiety, locked onto hers. "You won't believe what I found!"

She raised an eyebrow, intrigued. "What are you doing here?"

Jamie held up a rolled parchment. "This! It was hidden in one of dad's old books. It's a map, Lia, but not just any map. It's connected to Synchronos."

Unrolling the parchment, Lia's eyes widened in astonishment. It depicted the coastline but had intricate patterns and symbols she hadn't seen before. Along the edges, annotations in a language long forgotten provided cryptic hints.

Kael, joining them, leaned in to inspect the map. "This looks ancient. These symbols... they're from the time of the Founders."

Jamie nodded eagerly. "There's a legend Dad once mentioned. About an island that appears near Synchronos once every century. An island of untold treasures and secrets."

Lia, connecting the dots, gasped. "You think this map leads to that island?"

Jamie nodded. "Today's the day it's supposed to appear, at sunset."

The trio stood there, the weight of the discovery settling upon them. An island that appeared once a century, a map that might lead to it, and the setting sun as their time marker.

"We need a boat," Lia declared.

With the buzz of the town as their backdrop, they approached old Captain Morris, a sailor who was as much a part of the sea as the boats he helmed. With silver hair flowing down to his shoulders and a beard that told tales of countless voyages, the Captain listened intently as they explained their quest.

"Seeking the Phantom Isle, are ye?" he rumbled, eyes sparkling with mischief. "Many have tried, but few return. The sea has its own mind, and the island... it doesn't take kindly to intruders."

Lia, undeterred, pressed on. "Will you help us?"

Captain Morris stared into the horizon, seemingly lost in memories. After a long pause, he finally spoke, "Aye. But be warned, the journey will test ye in ways you can't imagine."

As the day wore on, preparations began in earnest. Lia, Jamie, and Kael, along with Captain Morris and a small crew, loaded provisions, navigational tools, and other essentials onto 'The Timeless Wanderer', the Captain's trusted ship.

As the sun began its descent, painting the sky with streaks of orange and purple, 'The Timeless Wanderer' set sail. The waters were calm, belying the mysteries they concealed.

Hours passed, and the coastline of Synchronos faded into the distance. The ship sailed through a dense fog that seemed to muffle all sound, creating an eerie silence. The crew whispered legends of the Phantom Isle—of treasures guarded by timeless sentinels and labyrinths that trapped the unwary.

Lia, gripping the map tightly, began decoding the symbols with Kael's help. Jamie, meanwhile, used an ancient astrolabe they'd borrowed from the town's museum, aligning stars with markings on the map.

Suddenly, a soft glow appeared on the horizon. It pulsed rhythmically, beckoning them. The ship sailed closer, and as the fog lifted, an island emerged from the depths. Lush forests, towering cliffs, and golden beaches—the Phantom Isle was a sight to behold.

The ship dropped anchor at a secluded cove. Lia, Jamie, Kael, and Captain Morris set foot on the island, a sense of anticipation in the air.

Following the map's clues, they journeyed through dense woods, crossed bubbling streams, and scaled rocky outcrops. The island was alive with the sound of exotic birds and the rustling of unseen creatures.

As night enveloped the isle, they arrived at a clearing with an ancient stone pedestal at its center. Carvings of celestial events and time symbols adorned its surface. Lia placed the map on the pedestal, and as Jamie aligned the astrolabe with the night sky, the stone emitted a soft hum.

A rumbling sound echoed as the ground shifted, revealing a hidden stairway leading down into the earth. Torches along the walls lit up, beckoning them into the depths of the Phantom Isle.

The underground chamber they entered was vast. In its center stood a magnificent crystal, pulsating with an otherworldly light. Around it, relics and artifacts from different eras were meticulously arranged.

Approaching the crystal, Lia felt a connection. She reached out, and as her fingers brushed its surface, visions flooded her mind. She saw the founders of Synchronos, the creation of the town, the forging of the amulet, and the island's guardians placing the crystal here.

Pulling away, Lia realized the crystal was a beacon—a bridge between Synchronos and the secrets of time.

As dawn approached, they made their way back to 'The Timeless Wanderer', the Phantom Isle once again shrouded in mist, waiting for the next century to reveal its treasures.

Back in Synchronos, their tale of adventure was received with awe. The town had yet another legend to cherish, and the trio—Lia, Jamie, and Kael—had etched their names into its history.

But more importantly, the bonds forged during their journey were timeless, echoing the very essence of Synchronos.

The heart of Synchronos was still aflutter with the trio's fantastic discovery when a woman draped in flowing garments approached them. She had deep auburn hair, an air of sophistication, and a countenance that seemed to belong to another era altogether. There was something timeless about her, much like the town itself.

"Ah, young explorers," she greeted with a musical voice. "I am Selene, the Keeper of Legends. I've been waiting for you."

Lia exchanged glances with Jamie and Kael. "Waiting for us?" she asked cautiously.

Selene nodded, producing a smaller, more intricate version of the astrolabe Jamie held earlier. "This astrolabe has been in my family for generations. It has always been said that when the time is right, it will find its match."

To everyone's astonishment, Selene's astrolabe began resonating in response to the one Jamie held, emitting a harmonious tone. The two instruments, ancient and steeped in mystery, connected across time and purpose.

Selene's eyes gleamed with excitement. "This is a sign. The isle you've discovered has more secrets, waiting to be unlocked. But only when the two astrolabes are brought together."

Jamie, ever the curious one, asked, "But why us? Why now?"

Selene looked at them solemnly. "Because time has chosen you. Synchronos exists at the crossroads of countless timelines. The island, with its treasure and mysteries, is but one piece of the puzzle."

The trio followed Selene to the oldest part of Synchronos – The Archives. A place where time seemed to stand still, it was filled with scrolls, books, and artifacts. And in the center of the room, on a raised platform, was an enormous hourglass, unlike any they had seen before. Instead of sand, it contained a swirling, luminescent substance.

"That," Selene gestured towards the hourglass, "contains the Sands of Time. It's not just an instrument to measure time but to navigate through it. And the island you discovered? It's the source of these sands."

Lia, realizing the gravity of their find, gasped. "So, the Phantom Isle isn't just a treasure trove. It's the heart of time itself!"

Selene nodded. "Every century, when the island emerges, it's an opportunity to replenish the Sands of Time. Without it, Synchronos and its unique relationship with time will be lost."

Kael, ever the logical thinker, queried, "But we've already been to the island. How do we ensure the sands are replenished?"

Selene hesitated, searching their faces. "There is one more secret. A ritual that needs to be performed on the Phantom Isle, only possible when the two astrolabes are united."

The group, realizing the monumental task ahead, began preparations. Under Selene's guidance, they learned the steps of the ritual and the significance of each gesture and chant.

The day of the next voyage dawned, clear and promising. The Timeless Wanderer was prepped once more, and with Captain Morris at the helm, they set sail, the combined power of the two astrolabes pointing the way.

The island, bathed in the golden hue of the setting sun, seemed different this time—more alive, aware of its significance. The very air was thick with anticipation.

Reaching the crystal chamber, the group formed a circle around the luminous crystal. Lia and Jamie, each holding an astrolabe, stood opposite each other. As they began the ritual, the chamber echoed with their voices, the crystal pulsing in response.

But as the final verse neared, an unexpected tremor shook the island.

Out of the shadows, figures emerged—The Sentinels of Time. They were the island's guardians, beings stuck between time, neither entirely present nor entirely in the past. They looked upon the group, not with malice, but with desperation.

"We have been waiting," one of them intoned. "The sands need to be replenished, but they also need to be protected."

Selene stepped forward, her voice authoritative yet gentle. "We're here to restore, not to take. Synchronos and the Phantom Isle share a bond, a destiny."

One of the Sentinels, with tears in his eyes, whispered, "We've been trapped, guardians for eternity. With the ritual's completion, not only will the sands be restored, but our watch will end. We can finally be free."

Moved by their plight, the group resumed the ritual. The crystal glowed brighter, and the Sands of Time flowed, filling the hourglass back in the Archives of Synchronos.

The island, having served its purpose, began its descent into the depths, waiting to emerge a century later. The Sentinels, with gratitude in their eyes, faded away, their long watch finally over.

As The Timeless Wanderer sailed back, the night was calm, but the air was thick with thought. They had achieved their mission, but at a deeper level, they had intertwined their destinies with the very fabric of time.

Back at the docks, as they disembarked, a figure approached them. It was Mayor Eldridge, but his demeanor was frantic, his face pale.

"You've returned! Thank the sands! Something's happened. Synchronos is unraveling!"

They rushed to the town square and froze. Buildings, people, entire sections of the town were flickering, disappearing and reappearing, as if being pulled in and out of time.

Lia clutched the astrolabe, her mind racing. The ritual, the sands, the island—had they missed something? Time was running out, quite literally. The fate of Synchronos hung in the balance, and they were at the center of it all.

Chapter Three: Echoes of Time

The town square of Synchronos was a whirlwind of chaos. Buildings phased in and out of existence, and people moved as if caught in a time-lapse, their actions repeating in a loop. Streets that once led to familiar places now opened to unknown vistas. It was as if the very fabric of time was tearing apart.

The trio, along with Selene and Mayor Eldridge, gathered in the Archives, trying to understand the calamity that had befallen Synchronos. The luminous Sands of Time swirled unpredictably inside the massive hourglass.

Jamie, ever observant, pointed out, "Look! The Sands aren't flowing downward. They're swirling in both directions."

Kael, connecting the dots, exclaimed, "It's not just measuring time; it's become a vortex!"

Lia, astrolabe in hand, approached the hourglass cautiously. A sudden jolt from it threw her back, and as she made contact, her surroundings shifted. She found herself in Synchronos, but it was different—both familiar and foreign. She was experiencing a memory, but not her own.

Young children ran past her, laughing and playing, and to her astonishment, one of them was a younger version of Mayor Eldridge! He was chasing after a butterfly, his laughter pure and unburdened.

Lia approached young Eldridge, reaching out to touch him, but as her fingers neared, the scene shifted again. Now, she stood on the Phantom Isle, watching as the Sentinels of Time performed the ritual they had recently undertaken. But something was different—a piece of the chant, a movement. It was an older version of the ritual!

The realization hit her; she was witnessing echoes of time, past events that had shaped the present.

Returning to the Archives, Lia shared her experiences. Selene, deep in thought, murmured, "The Sands are not just a measure but also a repository of memories. Every grain is a moment, an event, a decision."

Mayor Eldridge, recalling his childhood, smiled wistfully. "That butterfly chase was the day I decided to dedicate my life to understanding Synchronos and its mysteries."

Just then, a butterfly, identical to the one from young Eldridge's memory, fluttered into the room, circling them before settling on the hourglass.

A hushed silence fell over the room, each grasping the weight of the situation. The events of the past, present, and possibly the future were colliding.

Jamie, looking at the two astrolabes, had an idea. "What if we use these to tune the Sands, align them correctly?"

Selene nodded. "It's risky, but it might be our only chance."

Working in tandem, Jamie and Lia began calibrating the astrolabes, aiming to harmonize with the Sands' frequency. The room pulsed with energy, every surface humming and vibrating.

As the resonance peaked, Kael shouted, "Now!" and Selene began an incantation, older and more potent than any they'd heard before.

The Sands responded, their erratic movement slowing, then aligning, finally flowing in a harmonious rhythm. The hourglass glowed, casting a radiant light that enveloped the room.

Outside, Synchronos began stabilizing. Buildings solidified, streets returned to their familiar paths, and the townsfolk, freed from their time loops, gathered in awe and wonder.

Just as things seemed to settle, a ripple spread across town. People and objects briefly turned translucent, shimmering like mirages. Then, as quickly as it began, everything solidified. But certain things were... different. The town's statue now held a different pose, the bakery was on the opposite street, and most shockingly, Mayor Eldridge appeared a decade younger!

Kael, in astonishment, remarked, "We didn't just stabilize time; we reshuffled events!"

Selene, looking around, said, "The Sands don't just flow in one direction. Time, as we know it, isn't linear. It's a vast ocean, with currents and tides. Today, we've navigated its waves."

Lia, trying to understand the enormity of it all, asked, "But how do we ensure this doesn't happen again?"

Selene smiled, "Synchronos has always been a guardian of time. And now, with the knowledge you've gained, it's your turn to be its stewards."

As the day wore on, another unexpected revelation unfolded. The town's animals began displaying peculiar behaviors. Cats floated a few inches off the ground, dogs barked in slow motion, and birds drew intricate patterns in the sky as they flew.

Jamie, laughing at the levitating cats, remarked, "Looks like our time tinkering had some... fun side effects!"

The townsfolk, initially baffled, soon began to enjoy and celebrate these delightful quirks. Children raced against slow-motion dogs, and artists tried to capture the birds' sky patterns.

As evening settled on Synchronos, the town was abuzz with celebration. There was music, dancing, and stories—stories of the brave trio, the Phantom Isle, and the day time stood still.

Lia, Jamie, and Kael, standing at the town square, looked around, their hearts full. Their bond had grown stronger, and their place in Synchronos's history was cemented.

But as the night deepened, a cold wind blew, carrying a soft, haunting melody. The three, drawn to it, followed the sound to the outskirts of Synchronos, where an ancient, dilapidated portal stood.

As they approached, the portal shimmered to life, revealing an ethereal figure. It whispered, "The journey of time has just begun. Another realm awaits." And with that, the portal beckoned, its mysteries vast and unknown. The trio, glancing at each other, took a step forward, ready for another adventure.

The shimmering portal, with its haunting invitation, stood like a challenge. The moonlight cast eerie patterns on its ancient stones, and the ethereal figure seemed to dissolve and reappear, like a mirage.

Jamie, the ever-curious, took a tentative step forward. "We've come this far. How can we turn away from a new mystery?"

Kael, cautious yet intrigued, replied, "We don't know what lies on the other side. It could be another time, another realm."

Lia, holding her astrolabe close, said, "Synchronos has chosen us. We owe it to this town, and to ourselves, to explore every secret it holds."

The trio, united in their resolve, stepped through the portal. A sensation of weightlessness took over, and they were engulfed in a vortex of colors and sounds. When their feet finally touched solid ground, they found themselves in a place unlike any they'd seen.

Towering structures, made of gleaming crystal, soared towards the sky. Roads paved with iridescent stones crisscrossed the landscape, and the air sparkled, filled with floating orbs emitting soft, melodious notes.

As they took in their surroundings, they realized that the city's inhabitants were looking right back at them. But these were no ordinary citizens. They were translucent, spectral beings, moving gracefully, their forms continuously shifting between human and ethereal.

One of the beings approached them. "Welcome to Chronotis, the city of Time Spirits," it said, its voice echoing like a soft chime. "I am Eon, the Timekeeper."

Lia, gathering her wits, asked, "Why are we here?"

Eon floated closer, its form solidifying to appear more human. "Synchronos is the gateway, and Chronotis is the heart of time. The disturbances in your town were felt here. You've been brought here to restore the balance."

Jamie, eyes wide with wonder, whispered, "So, time doesn't just flow; it lives."

Eon nodded, "Every moment, every memory, they all reside here. And lately, there's been a disruption."

Guided by Eon, they made their way to the city center, where a massive crystalline tower stood. Inside, a swirling vortex of colors and images played out—the Tapestry of Time.

Eon pointed towards a section of the tapestry that looked frayed and torn. "This is the timeline of Synchronos. Something, or someone, has been tampering with it."

Kael, ever analytical, mused, "When we stabilized the Sands of Time, did we inadvertently cause this?"

Eon replied, "The Sands were a symptom, not the cause. Someone from Synchronos has been entering Chronotis, manipulating events, changing the course of time."

Lia gasped, realization dawning. "The portal! Someone else from our town has been using it."

Eon pointed towards the city outskirts, where another portal shimmered. "That leads back to Synchronos. But every time it's used, it destabilizes the Tapestry."

The group understood the gravity of the situation. They needed to find out who else was traveling between the realms and stop them.

Returning to Synchronos, they began their investigation. Clues pointed towards an old legend – The Timebender, a sorcerer who, unsatisfied with his destiny, sought to rewrite it.

At the town's library, hidden in an ancient tome, they found a shocking revelation. The Timebender wasn't just a legend; he was a past

Mayor of Synchronos! And with the town's memories reshuffled, he could be anyone.

Armed with this knowledge, they approached the current Mayor Eldridge. He listened intently and then, with a sigh, took out an old pendant—a time compass.

"Generations of Mayors have passed this down," Eldridge said. "It's said to resonate near the Timebender."

As they moved through the town, the compass began to pulse rapidly near an old, abandoned mansion—The House of Echoes. Legend said it was a place where past and future merged.

Inside, amidst the dust and shadows, they found a chamber filled with artifacts and a figure, cloaked in darkness.

With a dramatic flourish, the figure revealed himself, and to their utter shock, it was an older, twisted version of Jamie!

The older Jamie sneered, "I discovered the secrets of Chronotis and returned to reshape my destiny. But you," he glared at his younger self, "you still stand in my way."

Jamie, trembling but defiant, replied, "We make our own destiny, not by manipulating time, but by the choices we make."

The room charged with tension, a battle of wills played out. Lia and Kael, using their astrolabes, began countering the Timebender's spells, destabilizing his hold on the past and future.

As the climactic battle raged, the younger Jamie approached his older self. "Look at what you've become. Is this the destiny you wanted?"

Tears in his eyes, the Timebender wavered, the weight of his choices bearing down on him.

With a final, collective effort, they managed to seal the chamber, trapping the Timebender and his manipulations within, restoring the Tapestry of Time.

Exhausted, the trio returned to the town square, their bond stronger than ever.

But as dawn broke, a chilling discovery awaited them. The town of Synchronos, their home, had vanished, replaced by an endless, barren wasteland. Only the Portal to Chronotis remained, mocking them with its silent presence. Their journey, it seemed, was far from over.

Chapter Four: Shadows of the Lost Town

The vast wasteland stretched endlessly in all directions, an expanse of eerie stillness. Lia, Kael, and Jamie stood at its center, their faces reflecting a mix of shock and disbelief. Where once Synchronos stood bustling with life and mysteries, now there was... nothing.

Lia's voice wavered, "The town... it can't just disappear. We've been gone only a few hours!"

Jamie, his gaze fixed on the empty horizon, said, "Time works differently in Chronotis. Hours there could be years here."

Kael, ever the problem-solver, interrupted, "Speculating won't help. Let's check the Portal. Maybe Eon has answers."

Approaching the Portal, they were met by its shimmering guardian—Eon, the Timekeeper of Chronotis.

"You've returned," Eon's voice echoed, "and you've noticed the change."

Lia, her patience wearing thin, demanded, "What happened to Synchronos?"

Eon, floating gracefully, began, "Synchronos exists, but not in this timeframe. When the Timebender's chamber was sealed, it caused a ripple effect, shifting the entire town to another point in time."

Kael's face paled, "You mean we're in the future?"

Just then, a cat darted across the wasteland, its form familiar to Jamie. "Whiskers?" he exclaimed, recognizing the stray cat he used to feed back in Synchronos. But how could Whiskers be here, seemingly unchanged?

Eon's voice softened, "Time anomalies. Little fragments of the past that got caught in the ripple."

Jamie, bending down, scooped up the purring cat. Whiskers, despite the circumstances, seemed content in Jamie's arms, as if reminding him of simpler times.

Lia, taking a deep breath, inquired, "How do we bring back Synchronos?"

Eon pointed towards the distant horizon where a series of monolithic stones stood, "The Pillars of Epoch. They're ancient markers that can recalibrate time. To bring back Synchronos, you need to align them correctly."

And so, with a direction to follow and hope in their hearts, the trio, accompanied by Whiskers, began their journey towards the Pillars of Epoch.

As they navigated the treacherous terrain, they encountered pockets of deja vu—fragments of their past. There was the swing set from Lia's childhood, still swaying as if a child had just left it. Kael stumbled upon an old journal, the pages filled with his handwritten notes about Synchronos.

Midway, they encountered a roving caravan, but not of humans. To their amazement, it was a caravan of time-displaced animals—dinosaurs, dodos, and even mythical creatures like unicorns. And leading them was none other than Mrs. Everly, the town librarian, riding atop a triceratops.

"My dears!" Mrs. Everly exclaimed, adjusting her glasses. "I wondered if I'd run into familiar faces. After the town disappeared, I found myself amidst these lovely creatures. We've been wandering ever since."

Lia, her eyes wide with astonishment, asked, "But how?"

Mrs. Everly winked, "Oh, a librarian has many secrets. And a bit of time-travel was among the books I kept."

She handed them a small device, "This might help you with the Pillars."

Thanking her and promising to bring back Synchronos, the group continued.

The device, as it turned out, was a time-periscope. Peering through it allowed them to glimpse moments from different time periods. It was both entertaining and informative. They watched knights jousting, witnessed the first flight of an airplane, and even had a good laugh seeing a T-Rex trying to pick up a tiny feather.

Reaching the Pillars, they found inscriptions on each, representing different epochs. Using the time-periscope, they matched moments from history to each pillar, setting them to the correct timeframe.

But just as the last pillar aligned, a shadow loomed overhead.

A massive airship descended, its design a blend of futuristic tech and old-world charm. From it emerged a figure dressed in time-traveler finery—it was Dr. Tyme, a renowned scientist, and explorer of temporal realms.

"Ah, the heroes of Synchronos," Dr. Tyme exclaimed, his voice dripping with sarcasm. "Did you think you could just reset time?"

Jamie, clutching Whiskers, retorted, "What have you done with our town?"

Dr. Tyme smirked, "I merely borrowed it. A town that exists outside of time? It's a researcher's dream."

Kael, piecing things together, realized, "You amplified the Timebender's ripple!"

Dr. Tyme laughed, "Indeed! And now Synchronos is mine. But worry not, I'll send you somewhere... timeless."

Raising a device, he created a vortex, attempting to banish them to another era. But the Pillars, now aligned, pulsed with energy, deflecting the vortex back at him.

Caught off guard, Dr. Tyme was sucked into his own trap, sent spiraling into a time unknown. The airship, without its pilot, began to falter.

Using the time-periscope, Lia quickly found the controls, stabilizing the ship. "We can use this to bring back Synchronos!"

And as they set the coordinates, the wasteland below shimmered, reshaping and restoring itself. Buildings rose, trees sprouted, and the familiar sounds of Synchronos filled the air.

Returning to their town, they were hailed as heroes. But amidst the celebrations, Jamie felt a tug at his jacket. Looking down, he found a note.

"Meet me at the House of Echoes," it read.

As they made their way to the mansion, a soft glow emanated from the Timebender's chamber. Pushing the doors open, they were met by an impossible sight—an older Lia and Kael, who greeted them with a grave warning: "You've restored Synchronos, but the ripples you've created have repercussions beyond imagination."

Jamie stared at the older versions of his friends, his mouth agape. The older Lia and Kael seemed worn by time, their faces etched with lines of worry.

Older Lia approached, her eyes reflecting a depth of understanding. "We don't have much time. The choices you made today have caused a cascade in the Tapestry of Time."

Kael looked from the older version of himself to the younger, "What do you mean? We restored Synchronos, didn't we?"

Older Kael nodded, "Yes, but each action has a reaction. Your noble endeavors have fractured the time continuum in ways you can't imagine."

He gestured towards a wall on which images were projected. Scenes of ancient Rome being infiltrated by futuristic robots, the Renaissance era mixed with space travel, and the Stone Age bustling with modern cities.

"It's chaos," whispered Jamie, his eyes darting across the perplexing and startling images.

Just then, Whiskers, who had been playfully darting around the room, suddenly levitated, meowing with a distinct human voice, "The realms are merging! Oh, and can someone get me down?"

Everyone turned in astonishment, as the now-speaking cat floated in mid-air.

Older Lia sighed, "Another side effect. Animal and human consciousnesses are blending."

Setting aside the shock of a talking Whiskers, the group refocused on the dire situation.

"Is there a way to fix this?" Lia questioned.

Older Kael responded, "There is, but it's not without its risks. We have to visit the Epoch Nexus."

Jamie, with newfound confidence, declared, "Then let's go!"

But Older Lia interjected, "It's not that simple. The Nexus can be accessed by only one individual from any given point in the timeline."

Lia realized the implication, "So only one of us can go."

Suddenly, the ground shook, the vibrations intensifying. Through the window, they witnessed another Synchronos overlaying theirs, the two realities clashing.

Older Kael announced, "The timelines are merging faster than anticipated! We must make a decision."

Kael, taking a deep breath, spoke, "I'll go."

But Jamie shook his head, "No, I'll do it. This began with the Timebender and me. I have to fix it."

From a corner of the room, a familiar face emerged, Dr. Tyme. But he looked different, his demeanor no longer arrogant, but broken.

"You?" Kael spat, "What are you doing here?"

Dr. Tyme, his voice trembling, admitted, "I was trapped in an endless loop of my own creation. It gave me time to reflect. I wish to help."

Lia, ever the skeptic, narrowed her eyes, "And why should we trust you?"

Dr. Tyme pulled out a medallion glowing with energy, "This is the Epoch Medallion. It can stabilize the journey to the Nexus."

Older Kael suddenly doubled over in pain. As he straightened, his appearance began to alter, becoming an older version of Dr. Tyme. The room's atmosphere thickened with tension.

Everyone turned to the genuine older Dr. Tyme, who simply remarked, "It seems there are even more versions of me than I'd realized."

With no time to process this revelation, the group decided to act. Jamie, with the medallion around his neck, stood ready.

The Timebender's chamber began to morph, its walls undulating. The heart of the chamber revealed itself to be the gateway to the Epoch Nexus.

Before entering, Jamie looked back at his friends, "Promise me something?"

Lia nodded, "Anything."

Jamie, with determination, said, "If I don't come back, ensure that the mistakes of today are never repeated."

As he stepped into the gateway, a surge of energy enveloped him, transporting him through layers of time.

Inside the Nexus, Jamie found himself amidst swirling galaxies and neon pathways, each representing a strand of time.

A figure appeared, its form constantly changing - from a child to an elderly, from a bird to a lion. The embodiment of time itself.

"You are not supposed to be here," it spoke, its voice echoing.

Jamie, with the medallion glowing brighter, responded, "I'm here to restore balance."

Time pondered, "Your intentions are noble, but your actions were misguided. Why should I help?"

Jamie, taking a deep breath, replied, "Because I've learned. I've understood that time is a gift, not to be tampered with."

Time, after a seemingly eternal pause, nodded, "Very well."

The Epoch Medallion began to absorb the energies of the Nexus. "Once you step back, the Tapestry will mend itself. But remember, this comes at a cost."

Jamie, feeling the weight of the medallion, realized he was aging rapidly. The energy required for the mending was taking its toll on him.

Time spoke again, "A sacrifice for the greater good. Your youth for the world's stability."

Determined, Jamie activated the medallion, watching as the galaxies and pathways realigned.

Moments later, he found himself back in Synchronos, albeit much older. Lia, Kael, and even Dr. Tyme rushed to his side, relief evident on their faces.

The town was restored, the anomalies rectified, and time resumed its natural flow. Synchronos, with its adventures and lessons, remained a beacon of mysteries yet to be unraveled.

As they gathered to celebrate their victory, the shadow of a large bird appeared overhead. They looked up to see a magnificent phoenix descending, a scroll clutched in its talons. Unfurling it, they read the words: "Your journey with time is not over. The Age of the Phoenix beckons." The future, it seemed, held even more adventures for the guardians of Synchronos.

Chapter Five: The Age of the Phoenix

The town square of Synchronos, once a bustling hub of activity, was now adorned with banners and fairy lights. Children played in the corners, merchants peddled their unique time-wares, and laughter echoed. But at the center stood a massive statue of a phoenix, its majestic wings spread wide, and at its base, the cryptic scroll.

Lia, with a furrowed brow, examined the scroll. "The Age of the Phoenix... What could it possibly mean?"

Older Jamie, his silver hair flowing and wrinkles deep, mused, "It's a legend I had read about during my time travels. The Phoenix, a mythical bird, was said to have the power to traverse any timeline, unbound by the laws of time."

Kael, popping a grape into his mouth, remarked, "So, what? It's a bird that can time travel? We've had our fill of time adventures, thank you very much."

Whiskers, still occasionally meowing in a human tone due to the lingering effects of their recent adventure, nudged the scroll. "But this scroll appeared for a reason. We can't ignore it."

Dr. Tyme, having shed his arrogance and now seen as an ally, added, "The Phoenix's era is a convergence of all timelines. If it's beckoning, there might be a reason."

Lia interjected, "The Timebender's chamber! We can use it to decipher the scroll's age and origin."

The group hurried to the House of Echoes. The chamber, still vibrant with remnants of their previous adventure, hummed softly. Lia placed the scroll onto a pedestal, and a holographic screen emerged, displaying symbols and glyphs.

Jamie, using a magnifying lens, noticed a watermark of the Phoenix on the scroll. "Here! This matches the legend. The Phoenix was said to guard the Nexus, ensuring no entity misused it."

The symbols started rearranging, forming a clear message: "To the guardians of time, the Phoenix calls. When Synchronos faces its darkest hours, seek the Golden Feather."

Kael scratched his head, "Golden Feather? Sounds like a wild goose chase."

Suddenly, the chamber's doors burst open. Townsfolk, panic evident on their faces, rushed in. "The town square! It's changing!"

Rushing out, the group witnessed the sky darkening. Buildings faded, replaced by structures from different eras: Egyptian pyramids, medieval castles, and futuristic skyscrapers all jumbled together.

Dr. Tyme, his face pale, whispered, "It's the convergence. All timelines are merging into Synchronos."

Lia, determination evident, said, "We need to find the Golden Feather. It's the key."

With the town in chaos and time itself becoming unstable, they formed a plan. Jamie and Lia would search the annals of history in the House of Echoes for clues, Kael and Whiskers would scout the town for any signs, and Dr. Tyme would use his devices to stabilize the convergence as much as possible.

Hours turned into days, but their efforts seemed in vain. Synchronos was slowly losing its identity, becoming a mishmash of eras.

Jamie, pouring over an ancient tome, exclaimed, "Here! The Golden Feather is said to reside in the Temple of Aeternum, guarded by the Timeless Sphinx."

Lia, excitement in her eyes, added, "I've seen that temple! It was during one of our time adventures, in a desert landscape."

Dr. Tyme modified his airship to withstand timeline fluctuations. "We have to hurry. The Age of the Phoenix is nearing, and if the convergence completes, all of history might collapse."

Upon reaching the Temple of Aeternum, they were met with a massive stone Sphinx, its eyes gleaming with intelligence.

The Sphinx spoke, "To obtain the Golden Feather, you must answer my riddle."

Lia nodded, "We're ready."

The Sphinx began, "I speak without a mouth and hear without ears. I have no body, but I come alive with the wind. What am I?"

Jamie, after a brief pause, answered, "An echo."

The Sphinx, its stone lips curling into a smile, moved, revealing a chamber within. "Proceed, guardians of time."

Inside, atop a pedestal, lay the Golden Feather, glowing with ethereal light. As Lia approached, the chamber lit up with symbols mirroring the ones they saw in the Timebender's chamber.

But the room started shaking. From the walls, guardians crafted from sand emerged, their purpose clear: to protect the Feather at any cost.

Kael, swinging from a rope, managed to snatch the Feather. "Time to leave!"

As they fled the temple, the sandy guardians dissolved, their duty fulfilled.

Upon their return to Synchronos, they noticed the convergence accelerating. The town square, where the Phoenix statue stood, was now the epicenter.

Dr. Tyme, analyzing the Feather, remarked, "This is pure temporal energy. We need to channel it through the Timebender."

Lia, holding the Feather, approached the Phoenix statue. The ground trembled as time vortexes swirled, the Feather acting as a beacon.

The Phoenix, previously just stone, began to shimmer and morph into a magnificent, living creature of gold and flame.

It spoke, its voice echoing through all of Synchronos, "Guardians, you have proven your worth. Channel the Feather's energy, and I shall restore the balance."

With the combined efforts of Dr. Tyme's devices, the Timebender, and the Phoenix, the Golden Feather's energy spread across Synchronos. The converging timelines separated, each returning to its rightful place.

As calm returned, the Phoenix, its purpose fulfilled, turned back into a statue. The town, though weary from the trials, began to rebuild, stronger and united.

Days turned into weeks, and the adventures of the Age of the Phoenix became tales told around campfires. The guardians, their bond solidified, stood as sentinels, ensuring Synchronos remained a beacon through time.

Yet, one evening, as Jamie sat in his garden, an envelope, sealed with a phoenix emblem, appeared beside him. Opening it, he read, "Your journey isn't over. The realms beyond time beckon."

Looking up, he saw a tear in the sky, revealing a galaxy unknown. Synchronos, it seemed, was just the beginning.

Chapter Six: The Galactic Echoes

Morning dawned bright and clear in Synchronos, its first calm day since the Phoenix's rise. But for Jamie, calm was the last thing on his mind. The enigmatic letter with the phoenix seal and the tear in the sky revealing a new galaxy hinted at adventures beyond their wildest imaginations.

Sitting in his wooden armchair, Jamie pondered over the message again. The handwriting was unlike anything he had seen, almost as if the letters danced and shimmered, mimicking the stars.

Kael, in typical fashion, was skeptical. "A tear in the sky? Really? Aren't we done playing guardians?"

Whiskers, with a mischievous glint, purred, "Curiosity killed the cat, but satisfaction brought it back. I say we investigate!"

Lia, ever the pragmatic one, chimed in, "Before we jump into another adventure, we need to understand what we're getting into. What do we know about this galaxy?"

Dr. Tyme adjusted his monocle, a new addition to his attire, and said, "In all my travels, there's been a legend. A realm where time isn't linear but a vast ocean, with currents and tides."

Kael raised an eyebrow, "So, a time-ocean? And we're supposed to... swim?"

Before Dr. Tyme could retort, a strange hum filled the air, and a transparent portal opened in Jamie's garden, revealing a serene blue planet with rings of golden dust.

From the portal emerged a figure. Tall and elegant, with skin shimmering like the night sky and eyes that held galaxies within. "I am Selara," she began in a melodious voice, "Guardian of the Temporal Tides. We sent the message to you, Guardians of Synchronos."

Jamie stood, "Why?"

Selara hesitated, her starry eyes clouding, "Our realm, the Cosmic Echo, is in danger. Someone is manipulating the tides, causing ripples in time."

Lia questioned, "And how can we help?"

Selara looked down, her voice barely above a whisper, "We believe it's someone from your realm, a traveler who's misusing the Temporal Tides."

Whiskers, swishing his tail, muttered, "It's always one bad apple."

Kael, ever the protective one, declared, "Alright, so let's find this rogue traveler and bring him back."

Selara nodded, "But be warned. The Cosmic Echo is different. You might encounter versions of yourselves from different timelines."

With preparations made and Dr. Tyme's airship recalibrated for inter-galactic travel, the group, guided by Selara, entered the portal.

As they emerged, they found themselves floating in what seemed like an ocean, but instead of water, it was made up of shimmering waves of time. Beautiful and eerie all at once.

Selara explained, "This is the Time Ocean. Those waves are events, memories, moments. But see there?" She pointed towards a whirlpool, "That's a time distortion."

Kael squinted, "And our rogue traveler?"

Before Selara could answer, a figure emerged from the whirlpool, looking eerily familiar. It was another Jamie, but older, with a hardened face and cold eyes.

Lia gasped, "Jamie?!"

The older Jamie smirked, "Ah, so the Guardians have come to play. It's too late. I've seen the power of the Temporal Tides and I intend to harness it."

Jamie, shock evident on his face, stammered, "Why? How?"

The older Jamie laughed, "Why? Power, of course. With this, I can rewrite history, ensure Synchronos becomes the center of all universes. As for how, let's just say I've had a lot of time on my hands."

Dr. Tyme interjected, "You're destabilizing the entire Cosmic Echo! This isn't just about Synchronos."

Older Jamie shrugged, "Collateral damage."

Suddenly, the time ocean surged, waves crashing as various timelines started merging. Lia saw herself as a renowned historian, Whiskers as a grand sorcerer, and Kael, ironically, as a pacifist monk.

Realizing they had little time, Selara chanted an ancient rhyme. A bubble formed around the group, protecting them from the merging timelines. "We need to reach the Core of Echoes. It's the heart of this realm. If we can stabilize it, the rogue traveler's influence can be nullified."

As they journeyed, they faced challenges. Memories turned tangible, moments replayed with different outcomes, and emotions became physical entities.

After what felt like both a moment and an eternity, they reached the Core. It pulsed, vibrant and alive but chained and restrained by dark tendrils.

Older Jamie, wielding a staff made of condensed time, challenged, "You think you can stop me?"

Jamie, determination evident, responded, "We have to."

An epic battle ensued. Whiskers, with newfound sorcery skills, summoned temporal winds. Kael, tapping into his monk-like calm, tried reasoning, while Lia used her knowledge to decode the Core's rhythm.

Dr. Tyme, using his devices, and Selara, with her chants, created a shield, pushing back the rogue Jamie.

With combined efforts, they managed to break the tendrils, freeing the Core. Waves of time, instead of crashing, began flowing harmoniously.

The older Jamie, weakened, whispered, "You might have won now, but remember, time is infinite. I'll return."

Before they could react, he disappeared, leaving a trail of temporal sparks.

The group, exhausted but triumphant, returned to Synchronos, the tear in the sky sealing behind them.

Yet, as days turned into nights and nights into days, Jamie couldn't help but wonder: if there was an older version of him willing to wreak havoc, what other versions existed? And more importantly, what future awaited Synchronos?

Selara's parting words echoed in his mind, "Guard well the tides of time, for they are both a boon and a bane."

As the sun set, Jamie gazed at the horizon, aware that their adventures were far from over. The Cosmic Echo had given them a glimpse of the vastness of time, and the challenges it held.

Chapter Seven: The Timeworn Journal

Synchronos had returned to its rhythmic pace after the harrowing adventure in the Cosmic Echo. However, Jamie felt the weight of responsibility heavier than ever. As he looked out of his window at the ever-shifting landscape of their mystical city, he pondered the complexities of time and the vastness of its possibilities.

His ruminations were interrupted by a sharp knock on the door. Startled, he opened it to find a courier holding a package, marked with symbols from a bygone era. It bore the emblem of an ornate clock intertwined with an hourglass. The courier, without saying a word, handed over the package and left in haste.

Lia, coming downstairs from her room, exclaimed, "What's that you have there?"

"It seems to be a package. But this emblem..." Jamie's voice trailed off.

Whiskers, ever curious, purred, "Well, open it. There's no fun in just staring!"

Inside the package, wrapped in fine leather, was an old journal. The first page read:

"To the Guardians of Synchronos, If this journal has found its way to you, then the fabric of time is threatened once more. I am Prof. Lorian, a timekeeper from the past. My findings on time manipulations are in this journal. It's essential for the balance of Synchronos. Trust no one. Time can be deceiving."

Kael frowned, "Why send this now? And who is Prof. Lorian?"

Dr. Tyme, adjusting his monocle, shared, "Prof. Lorian was a renowned time theorist. But his works were deemed too dangerous, and he disappeared under mysterious circumstances."

Lia, flipping through the journal, noticed a peculiar page with sketches of various iconic landmarks in Synchronos but with subtle differences. There were notes scribbled hastily in the margins.

"The Fountain of Moments – not as it seems."

"The Clock Tower – hears the whispers of time."

"The Labyrinth of Echoes – where memories lie."

Whiskers, ever playful, quipped, "A scavenger hunt! How delightful!"

Jamie, a little more concerned, said, "It's not a game. If Prof. Lorian sent this, we need to understand why."

Setting off on their new quest, they decided to explore the Fountain of Moments first. An ornate structure, it was said that one could relive any memory by sipping its waters. However, upon arrival, they were met with a surprise.

The waters of the fountain had turned jet black.

As Jamie approached, he could hear muted whispers emanating from the fountain. Whiskers, being more daring, took a sip. Instantly, his eyes glazed over, and he slumped.

Lia panicked, "Whiskers!"

After a tense moment, Whiskers shook his head, "That was... unsettling. I didn't relive a memory. Instead, I was shown a future. A bleak one where Synchronos was in ruins."

Kael, ever analytical, pondered, "This must be a sign. A glimpse into what will happen if we don't decipher Prof. Lorian's notes."

Dr. Tyme, visibly concerned, remarked, "This is unprecedented. The Fountain of Moments was never meant to show the future."

The group, with renewed urgency, moved to the Clock Tower. Towering over Synchronos, it was a beacon of temporal stability.

However, as they neared, the once harmonious chimes of the tower sounded discordant, almost as if sending a warning.

Inside the tower, amidst the colossal gears and pendulums, they found another surprise. A holographic projection of Prof. Lorian appeared.

"Guardians," he began, "if you're seeing this, I have long passed. But my discoveries were too perilous to be left in the open. The Clock Tower doesn't just keep time; it listens to its very essence. Someone or something is causing disturbances. Find the Labyrinth of Echoes. It holds the key."

The projection flickered and disappeared, leaving them in stunned silence.

Lia, ever resourceful, said, "The Labyrinth of Echoes isn't just a legend?"

Dr. Tyme nodded, "It's believed to be a repository of all memories, past and future. But its location is unknown."

With the journal as their guide, they embarked on a quest through Synchronos, solving riddles, and navigating challenges. And finally, hidden beneath the very heart of the city, they found an entrance, marked with the same emblem as the journal.

The Labyrinth was unlike anything they had ever seen. Corridors that twisted and turned, mirroring memories and events. It was disorienting, as moments from their past played alongside possible futures.

After what felt like hours, they stumbled upon a chamber. In its center stood a pedestal with a crystal orb. As Jamie approached, the orb pulsated, and images swirled within.

It showed the rogue older Jamie, harnessing energies from various realms, growing stronger. Then, a scene of him confronting Prof. Lorian, who with great effort, managed to trap a part of the rogue's essence in the orb, rendering him less powerful but at a great personal cost.

The vision shifted to show the older Jamie, now in another realm, forging alliances, and amassing power, preparing to launch an assault on Synchronos.

Dr. Tyme, realization dawning, exclaimed, "We didn't stop him; we merely delayed him."

Lia, with determination in her eyes, said, "Then we prepare. With this knowledge, Synchronos stands a chance."

The group, united in purpose, left the Labyrinth, ready to defend their home, their adventures far from over.

But as they emerged, they were met with a shocking sight. Synchronos, once vibrant and alive, now seemed altered. Buildings were different, people unfamiliar, as if they had stepped into an alternate timeline.

Whiskers, surveying the surroundings, whispered, "Did we just travel through time or did time travel through us?"

Kael, gripping his staff, said, "We need answers. And fast."

Chapter Eight: Altered Echoes

The streets of Synchronos, once familiar to Jamie and his companions, now appeared different—almost distorted. Buildings that they remembered as sleek spires were now stout, brick-layered structures. The colors were off, too; the previously vibrant blue and gold buildings now possessed a rusted hue.

"Did the Labyrinth do this?" Lia asked, her voice quivering with uncertainty.

Whiskers, with his tail flicking side to side in agitation, replied, "I don't think so. It feels like we've been thrust into an alternate timeline. The essence of Synchronos remains, but its memory has changed."

As they ventured further, they noticed that the inhabitants of this Synchronos looked at them with confusion and suspicion. Their clothes were different, more reminiscent of an era gone by, and there was a palpable tension in the air.

Suddenly, a group of guards wearing unfamiliar emblems approached them, their stern faces showing no signs of recognition.

"You there! Halt! State your names and business," commanded the head guard.

Jamie stepped forward, "I'm Jamie. This is Lia, Kael, Dr. Tyme, and Whiskers. We're...well, we're from here."

The guard's face twisted into a frown, "Never heard of any of you. You seem out of place and out of time. You'll come with us."

Despite their initial resistance, they realized it would be futile to resist the guards and decided to follow them, hoping for a chance to understand the circumstances better.

They were led to what they recognized as the Council Chambers of Synchronos. However, instead of the familiar Council of Timekeepers, a single figure sat at the head of the room, a figure that they recognized all too well—it was an older Jamie.

Yet, this version was different. He was regal, dressed in opulent robes with a calm yet imposing aura.

The older Jamie looked at them with a hint of amusement. "Ah, the travelers from another timeline. I wondered when you'd arrive."

Lia, her voice steely, retorted, "Who are you? And what have you done with our Synchronos?"

The older Jamie leaned back, "I am Synchronos. Ever since I harnessed the power of the realms and solidified my control, this city has thrived. As for your Synchronos, it's but a distant memory, lost in the waves of time."

Kael, ever suspicious, inquired, "What did you do to the real Council of Timekeepers?"

The older Jamie smirked, "They were...uncooperative. Let's just say they've been given a timeout."

Dr. Tyme, piecing things together, deduced, "You've created a parallel timeline, one where you're in control. But why?"

The older Jamie, standing up to address them, said, "Power, Dr. Tyme. Unadulterated power. I've seen the weaknesses of our world, the infighting, the inconsistencies. Here, under my singular vision, Synchronos has never been more prosperous."

Whiskers, unable to contain his sass, remarked, "It's also never been this boring. Everything's monochrome. Where's the diversity, the vibrancy?"

Jamie, gathering courage, said, "We need to set things right. We can't let you dictate the narrative of Synchronos."

The older Jamie laughed, "And how do you propose to do that? This is my domain. You're powerless here."

Suddenly, the ground trembled. The walls of the Council Chambers shook as a resonating hum filled the room.

The older Jamie's face turned from amusement to concern. "What's happening?"

Dr. Tyme, with a glint in his eye, remarked, "Time. It's a fickle thing. Especially when there are anomalies."

From the corner of the room, the hum intensified, and out of thin air, a portal manifested. Out stepped Prof. Lorian, looking exactly as they remembered from the hologram.

"You!" The older Jamie snarled.

Prof. Lorian, his voice echoing authority, stated, "You may have tampered with the timeline, young Guardian, but you forget—time is ever-flowing, and it seeks balance. You're the anomaly here, and time has a way of correcting itself."

The room vibrated even more intensely as more portals began opening. Out stepped various versions of Jamie, Lia, Kael, and even Whiskers. They were all different, each representing possibilities from countless timelines.

The older Jamie, realizing he was outnumbered, shouted, "This isn't over!" He quickly conjured a portal and stepped through, disappearing from sight.

As the tremors subsided, the various versions began returning to their respective timelines, leaving the original group with Prof. Lorian.

Lia, trying to process everything, said, "What just happened?"

Prof. Lorian explained, "Time sought to correct the disturbance. By creating a nexus here, we were able to restore balance. Your Synchronos should return to its original state."

Kael looked pensive, "But the older Jamie, he's still out there."

Prof. Lorian nodded, "Yes, and he'll try again. But now, you're forewarned and forearmed. Guard the essence of Synchronos. Its diversity, its vibrancy—those are its strengths."

Whiskers, stretching lazily, remarked, "Well, that was an adventure. Do you think we could get snacks in this timeline?"

Everyone chuckled, the tension finally easing. The city of Synchronos, outside the Council Chambers, started shimmering and shifting back to its familiar form.

Jamie, feeling a weight lift off his shoulders, said, "We're home."

Lia smiled, "Yes, but remember, home is where the heart is. And our heart is with Synchronos, no matter its form."

They left the Council Chambers, ready to embrace their city once more, with the knowledge that their adventures were far from over. They had battles to fight, mysteries to solve, and time, as always, would be at the center of it all.

Chapter Nine: Stitches in Time

As the days passed, the streets of Synchronos seemed to have regained their vibrant pulse. The radiant spires glistened in the sun, and the melodious chimes from the Tower of Moments resonated through the air. Yet, for Jamie and his friends, a subtle unease persisted. The encounter with the older Jamie had left scars, not on their bodies, but on their very souls.

One cool evening, as they congregated in Lia's garden—now restored to its former glory with fountains dancing and blossoms emitting a sweet fragrance—Kael broached the subject on everyone's mind.

"We can't just wait for the older Jamie to strike again. We have to be proactive," he declared, tossing a pebble into the shimmering water.

Lia nodded, her face illuminated by the soft glow of the fairy lights that decorated her garden. "Kael's right. But how do we track someone who can manipulate time?"

Dr. Tyme adjusted his glasses, "We'd need to understand the essence of time itself. And for that, we'd need to venture to the one place we've never dared to go: The Timeless Plains."

Whiskers, licking his paw nonchalantly, inquired, "Timeless Plains? Sounds boring."

Dr. Tyme chuckled, "On the contrary, Whiskers. The Timeless Plains are where time stands still. No past, no present, no future. Just a vast expanse of nothingness. It's said that whoever conquers the Plains will hold the key to mastering time."

Jamie, feeling a newfound determination, asserted, "Then that's where we need to go. We'll train, prepare, and seek out the secrets of the Timeless Plains."

Over the next few days, the group underwent rigorous training. Lia's garden became their makeshift training ground, where they practiced mental exercises to strengthen their minds against the disorienting effects of the Plains. They also honed their physical skills, mastering the art of combat in a world where time didn't obey the usual rules.

Kael, with his warrior instincts, took the lead in training them in hand-to-hand combat, while Dr. Tyme focused on imparting knowledge about the intricacies of time manipulation. Whiskers, meanwhile, proved to be an unexpected asset. His sharp reflexes and keen senses provided valuable insights into detecting disturbances in the time continuum.

One fateful morning, after they deemed themselves ready, the group stood at the edge of the Timeless Plains. It was an eerie sight. The horizon stretched endlessly, with no landmarks, just a vast expanse of white, like an unpainted canvas.

Lia, clutching her staff, whispered, "It's so...empty."

Jamie squeezed her hand reassuringly. "We have each other. We'll navigate this together."

And with that, they stepped into the Plains.

Time seemed to lose meaning. The usual markers of day and night, sunrise and sunset, were absent. It was a perpetual state of in-between. Hours felt like seconds, and seconds like hours.

As they ventured further, they encountered riddles and puzzles, each designed to challenge their understanding of time. There were moments when the path behind them disappeared, forcing them to forge ahead, and times when they found themselves at the starting point, as if they'd been walking in circles.

However, their training paid off. Combining their strengths and relying on each other's expertise, they overcame each obstacle. They unraveled time loops, decoded cryptic messages, and battled figments of their imagination.

It was during one of these challenges that Jamie had a revelation. As he stared at a shifting sand clock, its grains defying gravity, he realized the truth about the older Jamie.

"He's a reflection," Jamie murmured, the realization dawning upon him. "A reflection of my fears, insecurities, and ambitions. He's not a separate entity. He's me."

Lia, understanding the gravity of the revelation, responded, "And to conquer him, you must conquer yourself."

With newfound clarity, Jamie approached the center of the Plains. There, amidst the endless white, stood a solitary, ornate mirror. Its frame was decorated with intricate designs of intertwined clocks and hourglasses, representing the interwoven fabric of time.

Gazing into the mirror, Jamie saw the older version of himself. The two locked eyes, the intensity palpable. But instead of hostility, Jamie projected understanding and acceptance.

"You are a part of me," Jamie declared, his voice resonating in the emptiness. "But I won't let you dictate my fate. I choose to write my own story."

As he spoke, the mirror began to shimmer, and the older Jamie's reflection started to fade. With a final, defiant gaze, the reflection disappeared, leaving just the image of the present Jamie.

The group, who had been watching in anxious anticipation, let out a collective sigh of relief. The vastness of the Plains started to morph, giving way to the familiar landscape of Synchronos.

They found themselves back at the edge of the Plains, with their city, in all its glory, stretching out before them.

Dr. Tyme, smiling with pride, remarked, "You've done it, Jamie. You've conquered the Timeless Plains and, in doing so, mastered your own destiny."

Jamie, feeling a weight lifted off his shoulders, replied, "We did it together. It's not just my victory; it's ours."

The group shared a heartfelt embrace, knowing that they had faced the unknown and emerged stronger.

As they headed back to the heart of Synchronos, the sun setting in the horizon painted the sky with hues of gold and crimson. The city seemed to welcome them back, its heartbeat in sync with theirs.

They had faced challenges, encountered mysteries, and journeyed through time. And while they knew more adventures awaited them, for now, they relished the present moment, cherishing the bonds they had forged and the memories they had created.

For in the ever-flowing river of time, it's the moments that matter. Moments of joy, moments of discovery, and moments of togetherness. And as the stars began to twinkle in the twilight, Jamie, Lia, Kael, Dr. Tyme, and Whiskers reveled in their moment, basking in the warm glow of victory and friendship.

Chapter Ten: Echoes of Tomorrow

The victory over the Timeless Plains didn't just signal a personal triumph for Jamie and his friends; it seemed to reinvigorate Synchronos itself. The city's citizens celebrated their heroes with jubilant parades and cheerful feasts, and the euphoria was contagious.

Yet, as the celebrations continued, Dr. Tyme grew pensive. One evening, he summoned the group to his sprawling study, a room filled with ancient artifacts, mysterious relics, and countless books on time theory.

"Welcome, young heroes," he greeted them, adjusting the chronometer on his wrist—a device that looked out of place, even in a city obsessed with time. "I've been reflecting on our recent adventure, and while I'm overjoyed at our success, there's a pattern emerging that I can't ignore."

Whiskers leapt onto a soft cushion and curled up, tail flicking lazily. "Do tell," he purred with feigned disinterest, but his alert eyes betrayed his curiosity.

Dr. Tyme pulled out a large parchment, the paper aged and brittle. As he spread it on the table, the group saw a detailed map of Synchronos, marked with curious symbols and annotations.

"Over the years," began Dr. Tyme, "there have been whispers of anomalies—instances where time behaved unexpectedly. We assumed these were mere quirks, but the emergence of the older Jamie suggests something more orchestrated."

Lia leaned over the map, her finger tracing a line of symbols. "These markings, they represent the anomalies?"

Dr. Tyme nodded, "Yes, and the pattern suggests that someone, or something, is trying to destabilize the very fabric of time in Synchronos."

Jamie frowned, "But why? To what end?"

Before Dr. Tyme could answer, Kael interjected, his warrior instincts on high alert, "Whoever they are, we must stop them. Synchronos is our home."

The old timekeeper sighed deeply. "That's where it becomes complicated. The source of these anomalies is elusive, and even with our recent victory, I fear the real battle lies ahead."

Suddenly, the chronometer on Dr. Tyme's wrist began to glow brightly, emitting a strange, humming sound. He quickly silenced it, but not before the group noticed his evident concern.

"That device..." Lia began, "I've never seen anything like it in Synchronos. What is it?"

"It's a Temporal Detector," Dr. Tyme explained. "It's meant to alert me of significant time disturbances. And it's never been this active before."

Jamie felt a chill run down his spine. "What does it mean?"

"It means," Dr. Tyme replied gravely, "that the destabilization is accelerating. We're running out of time."

The room grew tense. Whiskers stretched and yawned, breaking the silence. "Well, sitting here won't solve anything. We need a plan."

And so, they set to work. Hours turned into days as they researched, strategized, and prepared. Dr. Tyme's study became a hub of activity, with maps, diagrams, and tools scattered everywhere.

One afternoon, as Jamie was poring over an old manuscript detailing time rituals, he stumbled upon a passage that caught his attention:

"When the river of time is threatened, seek the Echoing Chamber. Only there will you find the answers you seek."

Jamie shared his discovery with the group. Dr. Tyme, stroking his beard thoughtfully, mused, "The Echoing Chamber. Legends speak of it—a place where the past, present, and future coalesce. But no one knows its location."

Lia's eyes sparkled with determination. "Then we find it."

With a renewed sense of purpose, the group embarked on their quest. They journeyed through the winding alleys of Synchronos, deciphered riddles, and faced challenges that tested their wit and courage.

Finally, in the heart of the oldest district of Synchronos, they found it—a door carved with intricate patterns of spiraling clocks, hidden in plain sight.

With bated breath, they entered.

Inside, the chamber was vast, its walls lined with shimmering mirrors of varying shapes and sizes. Each mirror reflected scenes from different moments in time—some familiar, some unfamiliar, and some entirely fantastical.

Whiskers, always the curious one, approached a particularly ornate mirror. As he did, his reflection began to morph, showing him as a majestic lion, ruling over a vast kingdom. He smirked, "Well, that's more like it."

But their amusement was short-lived. From the largest mirror in the center of the chamber, a figure emerged—a woman draped in robes of shimmering starlight, her eyes ageless and deep.

"I am the Guardian of Echoes," she announced, her voice resonating through the chamber. "You seek answers."

Dr. Tyme stepped forward, "We need to know who or what is destabilizing time in Synchronos."

The Guardian glanced at the mirrors surrounding her. "To understand the present, you must first confront the past." As she spoke, the mirrors began to glow, their reflections merging to show a singular scene—Synchronos, but in a time long past. The city was at its zenith, a beacon of progress and prosperity.

A man appeared in the reflection, a scientist, fervently working on an experiment. But something went wrong—terribly wrong. A blinding explosion rocked the city, creating the first anomaly in time.

The Guardian's voice echoed, "His ambition disrupted the natural flow of time. And now, echoes of that event ripple through the ages, threatening to unravel the very fabric of Synchronos."

Lia gasped, "How do we stop it?"

The Guardian looked at them solemnly, "To mend time, you must first mend the mistakes of the past."

Understanding dawned upon Jamie. "We need to go back and prevent the experiment from failing."

With a nod from the Guardian, they prepared to embark on their most crucial mission yet. But as they did, the Guardian whispered a warning, "Remember, in meddling with the past, you risk altering the future."

The weight of their responsibility heavy on their shoulders, Jamie, Lia, Kael, Dr. Tyme, and even Whiskers stood united, ready to face whatever awaited them in the echoes of yesterday.

As they stepped through the portal, the Guardian's words lingered in the chamber, "Time is a delicate tapestry. Handle with care."

Chapter Eleven: Tapestries and Threads

The pulsating portal opened up into a bustling marketplace. Vendors hawked their wares, children ran about, and the city of Synchronos gleamed, new and resplendent, in its prime. Gone were the traces of time wear and tear. The city was alive, vibrant, and unaware of the ripples in its future.

"Our attire," Lia whispered, realizing that their clothes stood out in the older version of Synchronos.

Before she could elaborate, a vendor approached them, "Ah, travelers from afar! Would you be interested in some traditional Synchronian robes?"

It was the perfect opportunity. Soon, the group was cloaked in garments that blended seamlessly with the era.

Whiskers, with a makeshift cloak that draped over his back, grumbled, "Why do I feel like I'm part of some theater troupe?"

Kael chuckled, "You look the part of a noble cat, my friend."

The city felt familiar, yet different. Buildings stood tall, untarnished by time. Statues that were mere remnants in their time stood grand and complete. However, the group knew they couldn't be distracted. They had a mission.

"Based on the vision from the Echoing Chamber," Dr. Tyme deduced, "the scientist's lab should be in the city's northern quadrant. We must find him before the experiment."

Navigating the city's streets, they finally arrived at a large building, adorned with clockwork and sundials. The sign outside read, "Chrono Innovations."

Lia hesitated, "Are we sure about this? Interfering with the past could have unforeseen consequences."

Jamie nodded, understanding her concerns, but his resolve was clear, "We need to ensure Synchronos has a future."

Entering the building, they encountered a bustling lab. Scientists and scholars were engrossed in their work, their faces a portrait of concentration. And there, in the center of it all, was the scientist from the Guardian's vision—enthusiastic, passionate, and dangerously close to causing the first time anomaly.

Approaching cautiously, Jamie called out, "Excuse me, sir?"

The scientist looked up, his eyes bright with curiosity. "Ah, visitors! How can I help you?"

"I... uh, we've come to discuss your current experiment," Jamie hesitated, unsure of how to proceed.

The scientist's brow furrowed, "How do you know about that?"

Before Jamie could reply, Lia intervened, "We've heard tales of your genius and wanted to witness it firsthand."

Flattery worked wonders. The scientist beamed, "Ah, well, you're in for a treat! Today, I'll be unveiling a device that can manipulate time—bending it, stretching it, reshaping it!"

The group exchanged uneasy glances. This was it.

Kael, thinking quickly, said, "What if we could offer an extra pair of eyes? Fresh perspectives? Maybe even help refine the device?"

The scientist seemed to consider this, then with a jovial laugh replied, "Why not? But first, introductions are in order. I am Dr. Chronus."

As the group introduced themselves, they began to work alongside Dr. Chronus, trying discreetly to find the flaw in his experiment.

Hours passed, and it was Whiskers, of all of them, who spotted it. A misaligned cog, seemingly insignificant, but with the potential to cause a catastrophic reaction.

Whiskers nudged Lia and pointed with his tail. Lia observed and whispered to Dr. Tyme, "That cog, it's misaligned. Could that be the cause?"

Dr. Tyme, after inspecting, nodded gravely. "It would create a domino effect, ultimately leading to the explosion we saw."

The challenge now was to correct the error without arousing suspicion. Jamie approached Dr. Chronus, "Doctor, may I make a suggestion?"

Dr. Chronus, engrossed in his calculations, waved him forward. Jamie, with a steady hand, realigned the cog, setting the course of time on a safer trajectory.

The moment of truth arrived. As Dr. Chronus activated the machine, a hushed anticipation filled the room. The device hummed, gears turned, and then, to everyone's relief, it stabilized, working exactly as intended.

Dr. Chronus, ecstatic, embraced Jamie, "I had a hunch you'd be an asset! Thank you!"

The group shared in the momentary celebration, knowing the fabric of time had been preserved. But they also knew they couldn't linger. The portal back to their time was unstable and wouldn't remain open indefinitely.

Taking their leave from Dr. Chronus and his team, they navigated back through the city. As they did, Jamie felt a tap on his shoulder. Turning, he came face to face with a familiar-looking young woman.

"Lia?" he whispered, stunned.

She smiled, a hint of mischief in her eyes. "Not exactly. I'm Liana, her great-great-grandmother. I've heard tales of travelers from the future, and I had a hunch I'd meet you. Take care of her, won't you?"

Stunned, Jamie could only nod. As they continued, he felt a deeper connection to Synchronos, to its past and its future.

The group finally reached the portal, its shimmering surface beckoning them home. One by one, they stepped through, returning to their own time.

Synchronos, once again familiar but now with a newfound vibrancy, welcomed them back. The tapestry of time had been mended, at least for now.

Whiskers, stretching lazily, remarked, "Time travel's exhausting. I think I'll stick to my nine lives."

Lia chuckled, "One adventure at a time."

And as the sun set over Synchronos, casting the city in a warm, golden hue, Jamie reflected on their journey, knowing that while they had secured their present, the mysteries of time were vast and unending. But for now, the echoes of tomorrow would have to wait.

Chapter Twelve: A Stitch in Time

The evening following their return, the City of Synchronos celebrated. The streets were lined with golden lanterns, casting a soft glow on the cobbled paths, while musicians played merry tunes and vendors offered sweet delicacies.

Lia, donning a flowing dress that shimmered under the moonlight, stood with Jamie by the Grand Clock Tower, the iconic heart of Synchronos. Whiskers, in a playful mood, chased after floating bubbles, his cloak trailing behind him like a superhero's cape.

"I can't believe we did it," Lia said, taking a deep breath. "It feels... surreal."

Jamie grinned. "Time travel has that effect."

Before she could respond, Dr. Tyme approached, his silver hair reflecting the lantern light. "The both of you, and Whiskers, have done a commendable job. Synchronos owes you a debt."

Lia smiled politely. "It was a team effort, Doctor. And besides, we did it for our home."

"And for the future," Jamie added.

Kael, with a goblet of sparkling drink in his hand, joined the conversation. "Speaking of the future, do you ever wonder... what's next? For Synchronos and for us?"

Whiskers, overhearing, quipped, "As long as it involves fewer jumps through wobbly portals and more fish treats, I'm on board."

Everyone laughed, but Jamie felt the weight of Kael's question. "We've seen the effects of meddling with time," he began. "But maybe the real question is, how do we preserve our future? How do we make sure this doesn't happen again?"

Dr. Tyme adjusted his glasses. "An institution, perhaps. Guardians of Time, who would ensure the integrity of Synchronos's timelines."

Kael nodded. "A blend of historians, scientists, and perhaps, adventurers like us."

Lia's eyes sparkled. "A school! Where we teach the next generation about our adventures and train them to be the next defenders of Synchronos."

Whiskers rolled his eyes. "Oh, great. More responsibility. Just when I was planning on early retirement."

They all shared a chuckle, but the seed of an idea had been planted.

Over the following weeks, with the city's backing, the establishment of the "Guardians of Time Academy" began. Housed in the very building of Chrono Innovations where their adventure had taken a pivotal turn, the academy was set to be a beacon of knowledge and exploration.

The curriculum was meticulously crafted, encompassing history, quantum mechanics, ethics, and, of course, practical training in temporal navigation.

Lia took the helm as the Principal of the academy, with Jamie as her deputy. Dr. Tyme was the Chief Scientist, ensuring that the lessons of the past were aptly communicated to the students, while Kael took charge of physical training, ensuring the young guardians were fit for any challenge.

Whiskers? Well, he got his wish. As the official mascot of the academy, he was showered with affection and treats, often found lounging in sunny spots or offering 'advice' to the students.

Months turned to years, and the Guardians of Time Academy became renowned throughout the land. Students from various corners of Synchronos applied, eager to be part of this elite group. Stories of the founding members—Lia, Jamie, Dr. Tyme, Kael, and Whiskers—became legendary tales, shared with reverence.

One day, as Jamie was walking through the academy's corridors, he paused before a large painting. It depicted their group standing valiantly, with the city of Synchronos in the background. The title read, "The Protectors of Tomorrow."

A young student approached, her eyes filled with admiration. "Sir, is it true? Did you really travel back in time to save our city?"

Jamie smiled, kneeling to be at eye level with the girl. "Yes, we did. But remember, it's not just about the adventures we had; it's about the lessons we learned and the future we're building."

She nodded, determination in her eyes. "I want to be like you when I grow up. A protector of time."

Jamie patted her head. "And you will be. Just remember to always respect time, learn from the past, and build a brighter future."

As the young student ran off, joining her friends, Jamie felt a deep sense of contentment. Synchronos was in good hands, and its future, though uncertain as all futures are, was bright.

That evening, as the sun set, casting a kaleidoscope of colors over the city, Lia and Jamie stood at their favorite spot, the balcony of the academy, overlooking Synchronos.

"Do you ever wonder," Lia mused, "if there's another adventure waiting for us out there?"

Jamie chuckled, "With time, there's always another adventure."

Whiskers, curling beside them, added, "As long as it's after my nap."

The trio laughed, gazing at the horizon, knowing that while their chapter was drawing to a close, the story of Synchronos and its guardians was just beginning.

Chapter Thirteen: Shadows of the Past

Three years had passed since the Guardians of Time Academy had been established. In that time, it had churned out scores of young, dedicated individuals, all bearing the mark of the guardians—a silver hourglass pendant. Lia, with her distinct leadership qualities, had shaped the institution into a beacon of hope for Synchronos.

Jamie often caught himself marveling at the progress, the students who walked the halls with a sense of purpose, ready to defend their city's temporal integrity. But while many things had changed, some remained the same—like Whiskers' stubborn refusal to attend the morning assembly or his propensity to sneak into the pantry.

One particularly chilly morning, as fog enveloped the academy, a knock echoed through Lia's ornate office door. Entering was a young woman with raven-black hair and piercing blue eyes, introducing herself as Elara. She bore no hourglass pendant.

"I come with a message," she began, her voice melodic but laced with urgency. "From a time far beyond ours."

Jamie, seated across Lia, leaned forward, intrigued. "Who sent you?"

Elara hesitated, then finally whispered, "It's complicated. All I can say is that there's a disturbance, a fracture in our timeline. Something...or someone is rewriting history."

Lia's brows knitted in concern. "We've encountered such disturbances before. They're dangerous but manageable. Our guardians—"

"This isn't like before," Elara interrupted. "The very essence of Synchronos is at stake. The past, present, and future are merging, causing chaos."

Jamie's heart raced. "How did this happen?"

Elara looked down, a shadow crossing her face. "An artifact. Called the Temporal Compass. It has the power to navigate any point in time, without the constraints of a fixed portal. In the wrong hands, it can rewrite history."

Lia's gaze hardened. "And who possesses this compass?"

A deep breath. "It's...it's me."

Shock reverberated through the room.

"I didn't mean to," Elara rushed to explain. "I found it on an expedition. But the compass has a will of its own. It yearns to create, to change. I've tried resisting, but the pull is too strong. And now, time is collapsing upon itself."

Lia's gaze softened, understanding the weight the young woman bore. "You came seeking help."

Elara nodded, tears glistening. "I cannot control it. But together, perhaps we can find a way."

An emergency assembly was called. Guardians filled the grand auditorium, their murmurs creating a soft hum. At the podium, Lia, Jamie, and Elara stood, the Temporal Compass between them, its golden needle spinning erratically.

Dr. Tyme, after examining the compass, announced, "We need to neutralize its power, anchor it to a fixed point. The Grand Clock Tower, perhaps."

Whiskers, lounging on a plush seat, mused, "Or maybe just toss it into a black hole."

Kael, ever the practical thinker, suggested, "What if we use the compass to travel to its point of origin and understand its creation? Knowledge might be our best weapon."

The idea resonated, and soon a plan was formed. Lia, Jamie, Elara, Kael, and Whiskers would journey to uncover the secrets of the Temporal Compass. Armed with the combined knowledge of the academy, they set out, the compass guiding their path.

Their journey led them to an ancient city, nestled between towering mountains and dense forests—a place where time seemed to stand still. The city, named Chronolia, was the birthplace of the compass.

In the heart of Chronolia stood a magnificent library, its walls adorned with countless clocks, each ticking in a unique rhythm. Here, they met the Timekeeper, an old man with a flowing white beard, his eyes twinkling with wisdom.

He welcomed them, "Ah, the guardians of Synchronos. I've been expecting you."

Lia, ever direct, asked, "Why was the Temporal Compass created?"

The Timekeeper sighed, leading them to a grand tapestry depicting the universe's creation. "Balance. The compass was made to ensure balance in the cosmos. But it was never meant to be used unchecked."

Elara stepped forward, guilt evident. "How do we restore the balance?"

The Timekeeper pointed to a constellation, shaped like an hourglass. "The Celestial Sands. A place where time is pure. The compass must be submerged there."

The journey to the Celestial Sands was perilous, filled with temporal storms and chronological anomalies. But with determination, the team persevered.

At the Celestial Sands, they found a cosmic pool, where golden grains floated, representing moments in time. Holding the Temporal Compass, Elara approached, her resolve evident.

"I'm sorry," she whispered, tears streaming down as she submerged the compass. The ripples it created seemed to resonate through the very fabric of existence.

A blinding light enveloped them, and when it subsided, they were back in Synchronos, the city untouched by temporal chaos.

The Guardians of Time Academy stood tall, students rushing about, the essence of normalcy restored.

Elara, her burden lifted, chose to stay, becoming one of the academy's most dedicated guardians. The tale of their adventure became a lesson, a testament to the fragility and importance of time.

Late one evening, as Lia, Jamie, and Whiskers sat on the academy balcony, the city lights shimmering below, Whiskers purred, "All's well that ends well, right?"

Jamie chuckled, "Until our next adventure."

Lia, gazing at the stars, whispered, "Time is endless, and so are our stories."

And as the trio sat, basking in the glow of their achievements, somewhere, in the vast expanse of time, another story was waiting to be told.

Chapter Fourteen: Secrets Within Secrets

Lia's dreams were always vivid, but tonight's dream felt real, tangible. She stood atop a windswept plateau overlooking a vast, mysterious land she didn't recognize. Massive structures, resembling clock gears, jutted from the ground, rotating slowly. This was no ordinary dream. She was in the Temporal Plains.

Suddenly, a deep, rhythmic voice echoed around her. "Lia... Time is but a shadow, a fleeting moment. What is lost can be found, and what is hidden can be revealed."

Startled, she woke up, her heart pounding. She needed to discuss her dream with Jamie and Elara, immediately.

The morning light filled the academy's courtyard, casting a golden glow on the ivy-covered walls. Students bustled around, engrossed in animated conversations about time anomalies and the importance of keeping the past, present, and future intact.

In her office, Lia recounted her dream to Jamie and Elara. They exchanged glances, a shared knowledge apparent between them.

"Temporal Plains," Elara whispered. "I've heard legends of such a place. A realm where time's secrets are stored."

Jamie interjected, "There's an ancient tome in the library, speaking of a 'Key of Shadows'. It supposedly unlocks the deeper mysteries of time."

Lia's mind raced. "Then we need to find this key!"

The trio, joined by Whiskers and Kael, headed to the academy's vast library. It was an awe-inspiring space, with towering bookshelves filled with tomes, scrolls, and manuscripts.

After hours of searching, Kael finally stumbled upon a dusty, leather-bound book titled "*The Shadows of Time*". Eagerly, they gathered around as he read aloud.

"In the heart of the Temporal Plains lies the Key of Shadows, an artifact of immense power. It unlocks time's deepest secrets, allowing one to navigate the currents of past, present, and future. But be warned, for the key is guarded by the Chrono Sphinx, a creature of legend, challenging those who seek the key with riddles of time."

The weight of their mission pressed on them. They needed the Key of Shadows. It was not just about the academy; it was about understanding time itself.

Preparations began. Equipped with tools, gadgets, and knowledge, the group, led by Lia, set off to find the Temporal Plains.

Navigating the unpredictable terrains of time, they soon found themselves standing atop the same plateau Lia had seen in her dream. Gargantuan clock gears turned, creating a mesmerizing dance of time.

In the distance, an enormous stone statue, half-lion and half-human, stood guard. The Chrono Sphinx.

Approaching cautiously, Lia called out, "We seek the Key of Shadows."

The Sphinx's eyes glowed, and in a voice that resonated with the weight of ages, it responded, "To obtain what you seek, answer my riddles three."

The first riddle was presented: "I'm not alive, but I grow; I don't have lungs, but I need air; I don't have a mouth, but water kills me. What am I?"

Whiskers, after pondering for a few moments, declared, "A fire!"

The Sphinx nodded, moving on to the next: "I speak without a mouth and hear without ears. I have no body, but I come alive with the wind. What am I?"

Elara thought hard, then confidently answered, "An echo!"

Satisfied, the Sphinx posed its final challenge: "What comes once in a minute, twice in a moment, but never in a thousand years?"

Jamie smiled, "The letter 'M'."

The ground rumbled as the Sphinx shifted, revealing a hidden alcove within its base. Inside lay a beautifully crafted silver key, encrusted with gems that shimmered like stars. The Key of Shadows.

But as Lia reached out to take it, a sudden blast threw them back. Emerging from a portal was a cloaked figure, face hidden in shadows. The Time Bandit, an entity they had crossed paths with before.

"Ah, Guardians, always meddling in matters beyond your grasp," the Bandit sneered, reaching for the key.

But the Bandit wasn't fast enough. Whiskers, agile and quick, pounced, knocking the key out of reach. A fierce battle ensued. The Guardians, united in purpose, drew on their training and the bond they shared.

In a decisive move, Lia, using a temporal gadget, trapped the Time Bandit in a slow-motion bubble. The Bandit's movements became sluggish, allowing Jamie and Elara to retrieve the key.

With the Bandit neutralized, the group returned to the academy, the Key of Shadows safely in their possession.

In the council room, the key was placed on a pedestal. Its aura radiated knowledge and power, a testament to the mysteries of time. Dr. Tyme, studying the key, proclaimed, "We must decipher its secrets, but cautiously. The balance of time is delicate."

Days turned into weeks, and the academy buzzed with excitement. Researchers, scholars, and students alike worked diligently, uncovering the mysteries of the Key of Shadows.

One evening, as the sun painted the horizon in hues of gold and crimson, Lia and Jamie sat on a balcony, overlooking the academy grounds.

Jamie, holding the key, mused, "Time is filled with endless possibilities. This journey has shown us just a fraction."

Lia nodded, a content smile on her face. "Yes, and there are countless stories yet to be explored. We're just at the beginning."

Whiskers, ever the opportunist, seized the moment to nuzzle against them, purring contentedly, reminding them of the simple joys amidst the grand adventures.

And as night blanketed the academy, the stars above whispered tales of time, waiting for the next chapter to unfold.

Chapter Fifteen: Echoes of the Future

Lia sat cross-legged on her plush, velvety bed, the Key of Shadows resting on her lap. The room was silent save for the soft ticking of a grandfather clock in the corner, a symbol of the journey she and her friends had embarked upon. An assortment of quirky gadgets lay scattered around her room, each one a memory of past adventures.

The key was not merely a beautiful artifact; it was a piece of history, a treasure trove of knowledge. Its ethereal shimmer beckoned Lia. As she touched its surface, images flashed before her eyes — ancient cities, magnificent creatures, and pivotal moments in time. She saw herself and Jamie, older and battle-hardened, defending a futuristic city under siege. Elara stood atop a floating platform, channeling energy from the Key to heal a tear in the time-space continuum.

Startled, Lia withdrew her hand. "Was this a vision of the future?" she wondered aloud.

Whiskers, ever perceptive, leaped onto her bed and nudged the key, his whiskers twitching. He looked up at Lia with knowing eyes.

"I need to show this to the others," Lia decided, gently placing the key into a secure pouch.

Racing down the spiraled staircases of the academy, her footsteps echoed through the marbled hallways. She reached Jamie's study, the door slightly ajar. Pushing it open, she found Jamie engrossed in an intricate diagram, plotting temporal anomalies.

"Jamie," Lia started, trying to catch her breath, "The Key showed me something, a possible future."

Jamie looked up, intrigued. "Visions from the Key? That's unheard of."

Elara, having overheard the conversation from an adjacent room, joined them. "What did you see?"

Lia recounted the vivid imagery. The three Guardians sat in pensive silence, the gravity of the vision weighing heavily.

"It's clear," Elara finally said, "we need to prepare. The Key is more than just a guide; it's a warning."

The next weeks were a blur of activity. The academy transformed into a hub of innovation and training. Students practiced advanced temporal techniques, and researchers decoded complex time scripts.

Lia, Jamie, and Elara underwent rigorous training, honing their skills, and understanding the deeper intricacies of the Key. They even developed a device that could harness its energy for defensive purposes.

One evening, during a routine practice session, the ground shook violently. The skies above the academy darkened, and an enormous vortex appeared, threatening to engulf everything.

"It's happening," Jamie exclaimed, "just like in your vision!"

Without a second thought, Lia activated the Key, its glow intensifying. She, Jamie, and Elara formed a triangle, focusing their energy on stabilizing the time rift.

From the vortex emerged cloaked figures, riding mechanical beasts. Their leader, distinguishable by his crimson cloak, dismounted, revealing himself to be an older, more menacing version of the Time Bandit.

"I've traversed futures and pasts," he announced, voice dripping with malice, "and in each, you Guardians are but a thorn in my side. This time, I end it."

Elara, ever the strategist, whispered to Jamie, "We need to use the new device, the Temporal Anchor."

Nodding, Jamie discreetly activated the device. It emitted a frequency, causing the mechanical beasts to malfunction, throwing the invaders into disarray.

Lia, tapping into the Key's power, created a protective barrier around the academy. Whiskers, energized by the Key, grew to ten times his size, furiously defending his home.

The battle was fierce. The air crackled with energy as time spells were cast and countered. But the Guardians, with the combined strength of the academy and the Key, had the upper hand.

With a final, concentrated effort, they forced the Time Bandit and his cronies back into the vortex, sealing it behind them.

The immediate danger averted, the skies cleared, revealing a brilliant rainbow. The academy, though scarred, stood strong.

In the aftermath, Dr. Tyme addressed the academy. "Today, we faced a threat like no other. But united, we defended not just our home, but the very fabric of time. The journey ahead is long, but as Guardians, we are prepared."

Lia, Jamie, and Elara, now revered as the academy's finest, stood side by side, looking at the horizon. Their bond was unbreakable, their resolve unshakable.

Days turned into weeks, and life at the academy resumed its usual pace. The Guardians continued their research, seeking to understand the future and their role in it. The Key of Shadows, once a mystery, now served as a beacon, guiding them through uncertainties.

In the heart of the academy, a new statue was erected. It depicted the three Guardians, Whiskers at their feet, the Key of Shadows held aloft. An inscription at its base read, "Defenders of Time, Protectors of Tomorrow."

Lia, gazing at the statue, felt a rush of emotions. The future might be uncertain, filled with challenges, but with her friends by her side, she was ready. The echoes of time whispered tales of adventures yet to come, and she was eager to meet them head-on.

Chapter Sixteen: Time's Whispered Secrets

The grandeur of the Time Guardian Academy's library was a sight to behold, rows upon rows of books that told tales of time's greatest adventures and mysteries. Its tall wooden shelves held centuries-old manuscripts and relics, while its lofty ceiling displayed the ever-changing map of the universe, the stars shimmering with every tick of the gigantic celestial clock mounted on one side.

In a corner, sitting by an intricately carved window that overlooked the vast gardens, were Lia and Jamie, deeply engrossed in a book titled "Synchronicities and Temporal Anomalies". Whiskers lay curled up beside them, purring in contentment.

"What does it say about the Key of Shadows?" Jamie asked, his fingers drumming on the table in anticipation.

Lia scanned the text. "It says that the Key has the power not just to navigate time but also to glimpse the myriad of possibilities that the future holds."

Jamie raised an eyebrow. "So, like seeing into the possible outcomes of our choices?"

"Exactly," Lia nodded, "But there's a catch. The more we pry, the more we risk fracturing the very fabric of time."

At that moment, Elara entered, her heels clicking on the polished marble floor. In her hand, she held a rolled-up parchment. "Look what I found," she said, unfurling it on the table. The parchment depicted the Key of Shadows, surrounded by a series of cryptic symbols.

Lia's eyes widened. "It's a cipher!"

Jamie leaned in closer, tracing a finger over the symbols. "I think these are instructions, perhaps a way to harness the Key's true power."

As the trio pondered over the cipher, the celestial clock began to chime, its sound echoing throughout the library. Suddenly, the Key, which Lia had kept securely in her pouch, began to vibrate. It levitated, its glow intensifying, illuminating the entire room.

Elara gasped. "It's reacting to the cipher!"

The Key's energy seemed to breathe life into the parchment, causing the symbols to rearrange and form legible instructions. "To witness time's whispered secrets, heart, mind, and soul must unite in purpose. When the past's regrets, the present's challenges, and the future's hopes align, the path will be revealed."

The trio exchanged glances. "It's not just about the Key," Jamie deduced, "It's about us, our bond."

Lia nodded. "We've faced the challenges of the present together, and we hope for a better future. But the past... what regrets do we carry?"

Elara sighed, "I regret not being there when the Time Bandit first attacked. I could've made a difference."

Jamie looked down. "I regret doubting myself, thinking I wasn't good enough to be a Guardian."

Lia took a deep breath, "I regret not understanding the weight of our responsibility sooner."

As they each voiced their regrets, the Key pulsed in harmony with their emotions. A portal slowly formed in the library, a swirling vortex that seemed to beckon them.

Without hesitation, the three Guardians stepped into the portal, Whiskers darting in behind them. They found themselves standing in an ethereal realm, where past, present, and future seemed to coexist.

Before them stood a grand structure, a citadel of time. And guarding its entrance was a familiar figure, the elder Guardian, Dr. Tyme.

"Welcome," he greeted, "To the Sanctum of Time's Secrets."

Elara approached him, "Dr. Tyme, what is this place?"

He smiled, "A place where time converges, where its most sacred mysteries are kept. You've unlocked the path with the bond you share, but to truly harness the Key's power, you must pass the trials within."

The interior of the citadel was a labyrinth, each corridor leading to a different moment in time. The Guardians faced challenges that tested their courage, intellect, and unity. From saving a sinking city in ancient times to preventing a future catastrophe, they relied on each other's strengths and the Key's guidance.

But the final trial was the most personal. Each Guardian confronted their deepest fears and regrets. Lia faced the weight of leadership and the choices she'd made. Jamie battled his self-doubts, while Elara relived the day she wasn't there to protect her loved ones.

Emerging triumphant, they found themselves in the heart of the citadel, where the very essence of time flowed. And there, floating above a pedestal, was another artifact, similar yet different from the Key of Shadows.

Dr. Tyme appeared beside them. "This is the Key of Light, the counterpart to the one you possess. Together, they maintain the balance of time."

Lia approached it, feeling its warm, welcoming energy. "Why show this to us now?"

Dr. Tyme's gaze was earnest. "Because a greater challenge awaits. The Time Bandit seeks both keys, and you must be prepared."

The realization was heavy. The battles they'd faced were but a prelude. As they exited the citadel, the Guardians felt a renewed sense of purpose. They had glimpsed time's whispered secrets, and with the knowledge came responsibility.

Returning to the academy, they shared their experiences with the other Guardians, preparing for the looming threat. The two keys, Shadows and Light, now lay side by side, symbols of hope and unity.

As the chapter closed, the Guardians stood vigilant, ready to defend time's sacred balance, their bond stronger than ever.

And in the quiet corridors of the academy, time whispered tales of adventures yet to unfold, awaiting the brave souls ready to face them.

Chapter Seventeen: Whispers in the Dark

The academy buzzed with energy as Guardians young and old convened in the Grand Hall. At its center stood a massive obsidian table, engraved with the insignia of the Time Guardians. The table's surface shimmered, displaying various points in time, some serene and beautiful, others chaotic and distressed.

Lia, now wearing the cloak of leadership, signaled for silence. "We've learned of the Time Bandit's intentions. He seeks not just to control time, but to reshape it, bending it to his will. With both the Key of Shadows and the Key of Light, he would become unstoppable."

Jamie clenched his fists. "We've faced him before. We'll stop him again."

Elara nodded in agreement. "But this time, we have an advantage. We know what he's after, and we've glimpsed the secrets of time."

Lia cleared her throat, drawing their attention. "Our mission is twofold. We need to safeguard the Key of Light, ensuring it doesn't fall into the wrong hands. Secondly, we must find a way to neutralize the Key of Shadows, stripping the Time Bandit of his power."

Dr. Tyme approached the table. "The secrets of time are vast and enigmatic. There are tales of a realm where time stands still, a place immune to its ebb and flow. If we can find this realm, we can use it to protect the Key of Light."

Jamie looked intrigued. "A place outside of time? How do we find it?"

Lia, deep in thought, recalled a story she'd read. "Legends speak of the Timeless Forest, where trees have witnessed eons yet never aged a day. It's said to be hidden, accessible only to those with a pure heart."

Elara smirked, "Well, that rules out the Time Bandit."

The group chuckled, momentarily easing the tension in the room. Whiskers, now sporting a miniature cloak, scampered onto the table, drawing everyone's attention. He sniffed the map, pawing at a spot marked by ancient runes.

Dr. Tyme's eyes widened. "The cat may be onto something. Those runes... they signify a temporal anomaly, a possible entrance to the Timeless Forest."

Lia grinned. "Whiskers, you've outdone yourself."

The Guardians sprang into action, preparing for their journey. They equipped themselves with chronometers, devices to track temporal disturbances. Elara brought along vials of sand from various epochs, useful for casting temporal spells. Jamie, ever the strategist, plotted their course, ensuring they avoided any temporal traps.

As they set forth, the landscape around them shifted, blending eras and histories. They traveled through medieval towns, bustling metropolises, and desolate wastelands, each a testament to time's inexorable march.

Their journey was fraught with challenges. They faced time-phased specters, echoes of events long past. At one point, a temporal storm nearly scattered them across different ages, but Elara's quick thinking, using the vials of sand, stabilized them.

After what felt like both moments and millennia, they arrived at the edge of a dense, verdant forest. The trees stood tall, their leaves shimmering in colors beyond human comprehension.

"This is it," Lia whispered, "The Timeless Forest."

Venturing within, they felt an odd sensation, as if time flowed differently. The forest was alive with sounds, from the chirping of ancient birds to the rustling of primordial creatures.

Deep within, they found a clearing bathed in soft, ethereal light. At its center stood a massive tree, its bark engraved with symbols mirroring the celestial clock from the academy.

Jamie approached it cautiously. "This tree... it's ancient, yet ageless."

Elara, examining the symbols, remarked, "It's a nexus point, where all timelines converge."

Dr. Tyme, his eyes filled with reverence, approached the tree. "The Heart of the Timeless Forest. If legends are true, placing the Key of Light within its trunk will shield it from any external temporal influence."

Lia, holding the Key of Light, stepped forward. As she approached, the tree's symbols began to glow, resonating with the Key. She gently pressed it against the trunk, which absorbed it, the Key becoming one with the tree.

A sense of peace enveloped the clearing. They'd succeeded. The Key of Light was safe.

Yet, their victory was short-lived. A dark portal opened, and out stepped the Time Bandit, his eyes filled with rage. "You think you can stop me? The Key of Shadows grants me power beyond comprehension!"

Elara, defiant, retorted, "Power without purpose is meaningless."

The Time Bandit, with a wave of his hand, unleashed temporal chaos, distorting the very fabric of the forest. The Guardians struggled, their surroundings shifting unpredictably.

But Lia, drawing strength from the Heart of the Forest, channeled its energy. "We stand united, as Guardians of Time!"

The combined might of the Guardians, bolstered by the Timeless Forest, clashed with the Time Bandit's dark

power. A blinding light enveloped them, the outcome uncertain.

As the light faded, the Time Bandit was nowhere to be seen, his influence banished. The forest returned to its serene state, the Key of Light's protection evident.

Dr. Tyme, catching his breath, remarked, "It's over. We've protected the balance of time, at least for now."

Elara, looking at the spot where the Time Bandit vanished, commented, "He may be gone, but he'll be back. And we'll be ready."

Lia, holding Whiskers close, nodded. "For every challenge time throws at us, we'll face it together."

The Guardians, united in purpose, exited the Timeless Forest, ready for whatever adventures awaited them.

And as they ventured forth, the Heart of the Timeless Forest pulsed gently, a beacon of hope and a testament to the indomitable spirit of those who protect time's sacred balance.

Chapter Eighteen: The Academy's Secrets

Back at the academy, the sun set behind an imposing tower, casting elongated shadows across the courtyard. Students milled about, practicing spells, discussing theories, or just soaking in the last rays of sunlight. There was an air of celebration; the Guardians had returned victorious.

Lia, Jamie, and Elara were gathered in a cozy room adorned with tapestries depicting heroic feats of past Guardians. Whiskers was curled up on a plush pillow, purring contentedly.

"There's something about the academy," Lia sighed, "It feels like home."

Elara smiled, "It *is* home. And after everything we've been through, it feels even more special."

Jamie, ever the practical one, was looking through some parchments. "While our victory in the Timeless Forest was significant, we must remain vigilant. The Time Bandit could resurface."

Lia nodded, "We should delve deeper into the academy's archives. There might be clues about the Time Bandit's past, his motivations."

The trio, fortified with determination, headed to the vast library of the academy. Towering bookshelves, filled with ancient scrolls and tomes, stretched as far as the eye could see. This was a treasure trove of knowledge.

Dr. Tyme, reading a heavy volume by the candlelight, looked up as they entered. "Ah, young Guardians. Seeking knowledge?"

Jamie replied, "We need to understand our enemy better. There must be something here about the Time Bandit."

Elara added, "And possibly about the origins of the Keys."

Dr. Tyme stroked his beard thoughtfully. "The library holds many secrets. But there's a section, deep within, that few have ventured into. The Forbidden Archives. It's said to contain chronicles from the time before time."

Lia's eyes widened. "How do we access it?"

Dr. Tyme handed her a silver key with intricate engravings. "This key will open the entrance. But be cautious. The knowledge within is vast and can be overwhelming."

Venturing deeper into the library, they found an ornate door with symbols matching the key. As Lia inserted it, the door glowed and creaked open, revealing a dimly lit corridor.

The Forbidden Archives were unlike any other part of the library. Instead of books, there were glowing orbs, each containing a memory, a fragment of time. Whispers filled the air, echoes of the past.

Lia reached out to one orb, and a vision enveloped her. She saw a young man, not much older than her, training as a Guardian. His passion and dedication were evident. As the vision progressed, she saw the same man, but older, disillusioned. He was experimenting with forbidden spells, attempting to control time itself. The vision ended with the man being cast out of the academy, vowing revenge.

Jamie and Elara, having witnessed the same vision, looked at each other. "The Time Bandit," Jamie whispered, "He was once a Guardian."

Elara shook her head in disbelief. "What could have driven him to such lengths?"

Lia, deep in thought, responded, "Betrayal, disappointment, the allure of power. There could be many reasons. But understanding his past gives us an edge."

Jamie pointed to another orb, one that pulsed with a dark energy. "This might give us more answers."

As they touched the orb, a whirlwind of emotions hit them. They witnessed the creation of the Keys. Two powerful entities, one of shadow and one of light, locked in eternal conflict. In an attempt to maintain balance, the Guardians of old had channeled their energies into two keys. The Key of Shadows was meant to be hidden, but its allure proved too strong, corrupting many, including the young Guardian they'd just seen.

The vision revealed the last location of the Key of Shadows before it was taken by the Time Bandit - a hidden chamber within the academy.

As the vision faded, the trio looked around, realizing they were not in the Forbidden Archives anymore but in a vast underground chamber. At its center was a pedestal, and on it, an empty space, the shape of the Key of Shadows.

Elara gasped, "The academy was its resting place all along!"

Jamie, examining the pedestal, found an inscription, "In times of dire need, when shadows overpower the light, seek the Guardian turned rogue. Only in reconciliation lies the balance."

Lia's heart raced. "We need to find the Time Bandit, not just to stop him, but to bring him back. The balance isn't just about the keys; it's about him too."

A soft meow echoed, and Whiskers, with his uncanny sense of timing, appeared, rubbing against Lia's legs.

Elara chuckled, "Guess he doesn't want to be left out of the adventure."

The chamber's walls began to shimmer, revealing another inscription, "The path to redemption is fraught with challenges. Seek the Guardian in the realm where time began."

Jamie mused, "The realm where time began... That's our next destination."

Lia, holding Whiskers close, nodded determinedly. "We've come a long way, faced countless challenges. But our mission is clear now. We need to find the Time Bandit and restore the balance, not just for the world, but for him as well."

And with renewed purpose, the Guardians set forth on their next adventure, the stakes higher than ever before.

Chapter Nineteen: The Realm of Beginnings

The path leading out of the underground chamber soon opened up to the fresh air of the courtyard. The sun, once on the brink of setting, now hung impossibly high in the sky, casting the academy grounds in a soft, golden hue. It seemed time itself had been disrupted.

"We need to find this realm where time began," Elara said, flipping open a small book she had pulled from her pocket. Her fingers traced the lines of the ancient text, seeking clues.

Jamie, gazing at the sky, murmured, "Time is a tricky thing. What if the realm is not a place, but a moment?"

Lia, with Whiskers settled on her shoulder, pondered Jamie's words. "A moment in time. The very beginning. But how do we access that?"

A sudden rustling from a nearby tree caught their attention. Descending from its branches was an ethereal figure, cloaked in shimmering robes. The Timekeeper. The academy's most mysterious figure, known to exist but seldom seen.

"You seek to tread where few have ventured," the Timekeeper began, her voice echoing with ages passed. "The Realm of Beginnings is not bound by space but by time. You must traverse the sands of past ages, confront the memories that shape the present, and face the uncertainty of the future."

Elara stepped forward, "Timekeeper, guide us. How do we embark on such a journey?"

With a sweeping gesture, the Timekeeper revealed a delicate hourglass, the sands within shifting and dancing as though alive. "This is the Hourglass of Ages. Through it, you can navigate the annals of time. But be wary; for in the Realm of Beginnings, time flows differently. A moment can seem like an eternity."

Taking a deep breath, Lia reached out, her fingers grazing the hourglass. The world around them started to blur, and a whirlwind of colors enveloped the trio.

They found themselves in a vast desert, the sky painted with hues of twilight. Towering dunes stretched out as far as the eye could see, and the air was filled with the murmurs of past ages.

Jamie looked around, "This... is the realm where time began?"

Elara, eyes wide with wonder, whispered, "The Sands of Time. Each grain represents a moment, an event. We're standing at the very beginning."

Suddenly, the sands beneath their feet began to shift, forming a pathway. The Guardians began to walk, with each step bringing forth visions of the past.

They saw the early days of the academy, the forging of alliances, battles won and lost, friendships formed, and betrayals that scarred the sands. And then, a familiar face: the young Guardian who would become the Time Bandit.

The sands played out his story: his unmatched prowess, his growing arrogance, his dabbling in forbidden magic, and finally, his exile. Lia felt a pang of sympathy. "He was one of the best. It's tragic how things turned out."

Elara, her gaze fixed on the unfolding tale, said, "It's a reminder. Power, without guidance or restraint, can lead to one's downfall."

As they journeyed further, the scenes shifted to their own adventures — their first meeting, the challenges they faced, their camaraderie, and the recent revelations.

Jamie chuckled, seeing a memory of Whiskers stealing a fish from the academy's kitchen. "Ah, some things never change."

Lia smiled but then noticed a set of footprints beside theirs. They were fresh. "Someone else is here," she whispered.

Following the tracks, they led the Guardians to a secluded oasis. At its heart was a figure, cloaked in shadows, gazing into the waters.

It was the Time Bandit.

He turned, his face showing traces of surprise. "You... here?"

Elara, taking a cautious step forward, said, "We've come to restore the balance. And that includes helping you."

The Time Bandit scoffed, "I'm beyond redemption."

Lia, determination in her eyes, countered, "No one is. We've seen your past, the choices you made. But it's never too late to make amends."

For a moment, the Time Bandit looked conflicted, torn between his past actions and the possibility of a different future.

Jamie extended a hand, "Come back with us. Let's set things right."

The Time Bandit hesitated, then slowly reached out, gripping Jamie's hand. The sands around them began to swirl, and the Realm of Beginnings started to fade.

When the Guardians opened their eyes, they were back in the academy's courtyard, the Hourglass of Ages cradled safely in Lia's hands.

The Time Bandit, or rather, the Guardian he once was, looked around. "It's been so long."

Dr. Tyme approached, a gentle smile on his face. "Welcome back, Arion."

Arion, the Time Bandit, nodded, "I have much to atone for."

Elara, placing a reassuring hand on his shoulder, said, "We'll face the future together. As Guardians."

As the sun began to set, the academy stood united, its pillars stronger than ever, ready to face whatever challenges lay ahead.

Chapter Twenty: Echoes of Yesterday

The gentle murmur of a bubbling brook was the first sound Arion heard the following morning. Opening his eyes, he found himself lying on soft grass under a canopy of willow trees. The sun's rays peeked through the branches, creating dappled patterns on the ground. It was the same grove he and his friends used to frequent as young Guardians-in-training.

Sitting up, he noticed the academy in the distance, its imposing towers rising proudly against the horizon. Time felt warped, both the distant past and the present converging in this tranquil space.

Walking toward the brook, Arion knelt and splashed cold water on his face, memories rushing back. He remembered racing with Jamie, Elara besting him in their practice duels, and Lia's laughter ringing through the air as they shared secrets by the fire.

A rustling sound drew his attention, and out of the underbrush emerged a rabbit. But not just any rabbit — it was Whiskers, but much younger, without the tuft of gray fur he now sported on his chin.

Amazed, Arion whispered, "Is this... a memory?"

Whiskers, ever the mischief-maker, grabbed a piece of parchment from Arion's pocket and darted away.

"Hey! Get back here!" Arion shouted playfully, giving chase.

Rounding a bend, he was no longer following young Whiskers but instead stumbled upon a scene from his past — a younger version of himself sitting with Jamie, Elara, and Lia, the four of them pouring over maps and scrolls.

They seemed to be planning some sort of mission, their voices filled with enthusiasm and determination.

"You sure this is where the relic is hidden?" young Lia asked, pointing to a spot on the map.

"It has to be," young Elara responded. "The legends align with this location."

Young Jamie grinned, "Then let's retrieve it before it falls into the wrong hands."

Young Arion nodded, determination in his eyes. "We'll succeed. Together."

The memory faded, replaced by another. Arion now found himself on a rocky outcrop, a storm brewing in the distance. Beside him stood a cloaked figure — his mentor, the previous Timekeeper.

"Do you understand the responsibility you bear, Arion?" the Timekeeper asked, her voice heavy with gravitas.

Arion, younger and more naive, nodded, "I do. And I won't let you down."

The Timekeeper gazed into the distance. "Time is fragile. Guard it well."

The scenes shifted rapidly, showing the downward spiral of Arion's choices, his transformation into the Time Bandit, his confrontation with his friends, and his exile.

The final scene was the most poignant: Arion, alone, surrounded by the very sands of time he sought to control, imprisoned by his own ambition.

The grove faded away, replaced by the familiar walls of Arion's room in the academy. It was all a dream — a reflection on the past.

Arion sat up, his heart heavy. The echoes of yesterday were powerful reminders of the journey he had undertaken and the choices he had made.

There was a knock on the door. "Come in," Arion called.

Elara stepped inside, her face softening upon seeing him. "How are you feeling?"

Arion hesitated, searching for the right words. "Reflective," he finally said.

Elara sat beside him. "Your past doesn't define you, Arion. We believe in the Guardian you once were and can be again."

Arion smiled gratefully. "Thank you, Elara."

As they sat in comfortable silence, Arion felt a renewed sense of purpose. He had a chance to rewrite his legacy, and he was determined to seize it.

The following weeks saw Arion re-integrating into the academy. He underwent rigorous training to regain his skills, participated in missions, and rebuilt relationships.

Lia, ever the compassionate soul, often sat with him, sharing tales of their adventures during his absence and offering guidance.

Jamie, initially wary, slowly began to trust Arion again. Their bond, once unbreakable, was on the mend.

One day, as Arion walked through the academy's grand library, he stumbled upon a hidden section — the Time Archives. It was here that all records related to time magic were stored.

Curiosity piqued, Arion began researching, hoping to find a way to safeguard time from future threats.

Days turned into weeks, and one evening, as the sun set, Arion made a breakthrough. He found an ancient spell capable of sealing the time rifts, preventing any misuse.

Gathering Jamie, Elara, and Lia, they performed the ritual. The academy grounds shimmered, and the very fabric of time solidified, making it impervious to manipulation.

The four Guardians, standing united, watched as the final rift sealed. The threat of time being altered was no more.

Arion turned to his friends, tears in his eyes. "Thank you. For giving me a second chance."

Lia smiled warmly. "That's what family does."

Elara nodded, "The past is behind us. It's the future we must focus on."

Jamie clasped Arion's shoulder. "Together, as Guardians."

Arion, looking at the academy and the world beyond, felt hope. The legacy of the Guardians was secure, and while challenges would arise, they would face them united.

But as the day gave way to night, a shadowy figure watched from a distance, a sinister grin forming. The story was far from over.

Chapter Twenty One: Whispers of Shadows

The sun was just beginning to dip below the horizon, casting a golden hue over the academy grounds. Birds chirped their evening song, and a gentle breeze rustled the leaves. It was a picture of serenity, a calm that had been hard-won.

In the center of the courtyard, a marble statue of the first Timekeeper stood tall, a reminder of the legacy the Guardians upheld. At its base, children of the academy played, their laughter echoing with innocence and joy. Among them was little Tommy, his dark hair bouncing as he raced after his friends, pretending to control time with every exaggerated hand wave.

Watching from a nearby bench were Arion and Jamie, their expressions a mixture of nostalgia and contentment.

"Do you remember when we were that young, thinking time was something we could just play with?" Jamie mused, a wistful smile on his face.

Arion chuckled, "We were naive. But it's that innocence, that belief in the impossible, that shapes us."

The two lapsed into comfortable silence, watching the children play. However, the peace was interrupted by a soft whisper, almost like a shadowy breeze, that tickled Arion's ear.

Time bends to no one... but shadows can.

Arion stiffened, looking around. "Did you hear that?"

Jamie frowned, "Hear what?"

Arion shook his head, trying to dismiss the unsettling feeling. "Never mind. Probably just the wind."

But as the evening progressed, Arion couldn't shake off the sensation of being watched. He began to see fleeting shadows out of the corner of his eye, only for them to vanish when he tried to focus.

Dinner that evening was a lively affair. The Guardians, instructors, and students all gathered in the grand dining hall, feasting and sharing stories.

Lia, ever the storyteller, recounted a recent mission where she and a group of young Guardians had outsmarted a gang of rogue magicians. Elara, sitting beside her, playfully exaggerated every detail, drawing peals of laughter from the audience.

Amidst the merriment, Arion felt a cold draft. Glancing toward the window, he saw a dark figure, its form indistinct, like a wisp of smoke. Their eyes locked, and the figure gestured for him to come.

Pushing back his chair, Arion excused himself and cautiously approached the window. However, once outside, the shadowy figure was nowhere to be seen.

"Looking for someone?" a voice echoed.

Arion whirled around, his Guardian instincts on high alert. "Who are you? Show yourself!"

A swirl of darkness materialized before him, condensing into the form of a tall, cloaked figure. "I am a mere messenger," the figure replied, its voice dripping with mystery. "A harbinger of what's to come."

Arion frowned, "Speak clearly. What do you want?"

The shadowy figure chuckled, "Time is not the only force that yearns to be free. Shadows, too, have their desires. And while you may have sealed the rifts of time, you cannot escape the grasp of the shadows."

Before Arion could react, the figure vanished, leaving only a chilling breeze in its wake.

Rushing back inside, Arion shared his encounter with Jamie, Elara, and Lia.

"Shadows? Are they another faction of magic we're unaware of?" Lia pondered.

Elara frowned, "In the ancient texts, there's mention of Shadowmancers — sorcerers who drew power from the darkness. But I thought they were mere legends."

Jamie grunted, "Seems like these legends have a way of coming to life lately."

The quartet decided to delve into the academy's archives, hoping to find more information on these elusive Shadowmancers.

Hours turned into days as they sifted through ancient scrolls and manuscripts. Lia, her fingers stained with ink, finally stumbled upon a lead.

"Listen to this," she began, reading from a weathered tome. "In the Age of Twilight, when day meets night, the Shadowmancers rose. Drawing power from the obsidian heart, they sought to blanket the world in eternal darkness. Only by the light of the silver moon were they defeated and banished."

Elara, her brow furrowed, mused, "The obsidian heart... I've come across that term before. It's said to be a powerful artifact, the source of all shadow magic."

Arion sighed, "So, we have another powerful group wanting to plunge the world into chaos."

Jamie smirked, "Guess our work is never done."

Determined, the Guardians devised a plan. Using the academy's resources, they located the rumored resting place of the obsidian heart — a hidden cavern deep within the Whispering Woods.

Journeying together, they navigated treacherous terrains, facing both natural and magical obstacles. Yet, with each challenge, their bond only grew stronger.

Deep within the cavern, they discovered the obsidian heart, pulsating with dark energy. However, guarding it were the Shadowmancers, their forms fluid and ever-changing.

A fierce battle ensued. Arion, drawing upon

his Timekeeper abilities, sought to slow the relentless assault. Jamie, with his martial prowess, kept the Shadowmancers at bay. Lia and Elara combined their magic, casting radiant spells that pierced the darkness.

As the battle reached its climax, the Guardians realized the key was not to defeat the shadows but to contain them. Using a spell from the ancient tome, they sealed the obsidian heart, trapping the Shadowmancers once more.

Exhausted but victorious, the Guardians returned to the academy, the threat of shadows quelled for now.

That evening, as they celebrated their triumph, Arion looked out at the setting sun, pondering the delicate balance between light and dark.

"To every shadow, there's a source of light," he whispered, his friends nodding in agreement.

And while the future was uncertain, they faced it united, ever vigilant against the lurking shadows.

Chapter Twenty-Two: The Dawn of Equilibrium

The sun stretched across the horizon, painting the academy with hues of oranges and purples. It had been several weeks since the encounter with the Shadowmancers, and the academy grounds buzzed with an energy of relief and joy. Everywhere one looked, students practiced their arts, their expressions carefree and laughter abundant.

In the heart of this serene panorama, under the shade of a massive oak tree, the Guardians sat in a circle. Lia had a scroll unfurled on her lap, the details of their recent adventure inked meticulously in her elegant handwriting. Arion, Jamie, and Elara listened intently, occasionally interrupting with humorous anecdotes or corrections.

"The tale of light and shadow," Elara mused, tracing her finger over the sketch of the obsidian heart. "It's like an eternal dance, isn't it?"

Jamie grinned, taking a bite from an apple. "Well, every dance has its rhythm. The trick is not to let one partner dominate the other."

Lia looked up thoughtfully. "It's about balance, isn't it? Neither light nor shadow can exist without the other. They coexist, each defining the other."

Arion nodded, "Our journey has taught us the value of that equilibrium. The rifts of time, the magic we wield, the challenges we faced with the Shadowmancers—it all points to the delicate harmony of the universe."

The group lapsed into contemplative silence, the weight of their shared experiences hanging in the air.

After a while, Tommy, who had been playing nearby, raced towards them, his face alight with excitement. "Guardian Arion! Look what I found!" He presented a small, translucent crystal, its surface emitting a soft glow.

Arion took the crystal, examining it closely. "It's a moonstone," he whispered in awe. "They're incredibly rare, said to contain the essence of the silver moon."

Tommy's eyes widened. "Really? I just thought it was pretty."

Elara chuckled, ruffling Tommy's hair. "Sometimes, the most extraordinary things appear in the simplest of forms."

Taking a deep breath, Arion stood up and faced his companions. "We've been through so much together, faced insurmountable odds, and yet here we are. But our journey isn't about the challenges; it's about the lessons we've learned and the bonds we've forged."

Jamie smirked, "Sounds like the beginning of another epic tale."

Lia smiled, rolling up her scroll. "Every end is a new beginning, after all."

The evening sun cast elongated shadows as the Guardians made their way to the central courtyard. At its heart stood the marble statue of the first Timekeeper, the very symbol of their legacy. Placing the moonstone at the statue's base, Arion whispered an incantation.

The stone absorbed the last rays of the setting sun, shimmering brilliantly before releasing a beam of light that shot up into the twilight sky. As the beam made contact with the first stars of the evening, the entire academy was bathed in a soft silver glow, symbolizing the union of day and night.

Students and instructors gathered, their faces upturned in wonder. The light from the moonstone pulsed, its rhythm harmonizing with the heartbeats of all present, uniting them in a moment of shared reverence.

As the glow slowly faded, a feeling of contentment enveloped the academy. Every individual felt connected, not just to each other, but to the universe itself.

Later that night, as the Guardians sat around a campfire, Jamie strummed a lighthearted tune on his guitar. Elara and Lia, their voices blending perfectly, sang of adventures and friendships. Arion, looking up at the vast expanse of the starry sky, felt a profound sense of peace.

The journey had been long, filled with trials and tribulations. But as the flames danced and the music played, there was a unanimous realization—they had found their balance.

The balance between past and future, magic and reality, light and shadow. A balance that wasn't just about combating external forces but understanding oneself.

And as the fire reduced to embers, and the first rays of dawn painted the sky, the academy, with its Guardians and students, stood as a beacon—a testament to the enduring spirit of unity, understanding, and harmony.

In the dance of light and shadow, they had found their rhythm, and with it, the promise of a future filled with endless possibilities.

The End

Epilogue: The Gentle Pull of Time

Three years later...

Lia stood atop a hill, looking over the thriving metropolis below, where winding streets intertwined with sparkling waterways. The once-desolate Shadowlands had transformed, bearing little resemblance to the dark realm they once knew. The merger of the realms, though fraught with initial chaos, had birthed a place of balance—a realm where light and dark, past and present, danced in harmonious rhythm.

Beside her, Jamie strummed his guitar, playing a soft tune, echoing the sentiment of the place. His songs had become an integral part of the new world's culture, weaving tales of their adventures and teaching new generations about the importance of unity and balance.

Elara, in her usual enigmatic fashion, was in and out of the shadows, ensuring that the delicate equilibrium between the realms remained intact. Though no one said it aloud, everyone knew that she was the unsung sentinel, the quiet guardian who watched over the spaces in between.

And Arion, true to his Guardian vow, had established an institution that educated the young about the power of time. No longer hidden, the Timekeeper Academy stood proud, its spires glistening in the sun, a beacon of hope for the future.

Together, the four of them had played their parts in reshaping their world. The burdens of the past had lightened, replaced by the promises of the future. Yet, amidst all the change, one constant remained—their unbreakable bond.

As the sun began its descent, painting the sky with hues of pink and gold, Lia pulled out the ancient Timekeeper's tome, its pages now filled with their adventures. It was a testament to their journey, a story that had begun with uncertainty but ended in unity.

"Think there's more to add?" Jamie asked with a playful grin.

Lia smiled, her eyes misting over. "Every ending is a new beginning," she whispered, closing the book.

And as the first star twinkled in the twilight, somewhere, in a corner of the merged realms, a clock ticked, its gentle rhythm signaling the continuation of time's eternal dance. The world moved on, but the legacy of the Guardians would forever remain, etched in the sands of time.